CH00346690

CHERISHED

The Mountain Man's Babies

FRANKIE LOVE

Frankie Love

COPYRIGHT

CHAPTER ONE

Cherish

When we were four, I made him a mud pie and he told me I was as sweet as his mama's lemonade.

When we were seven, we sang in the choir together and he held my song book and I told him his voice was as clear and beautiful as a sunny day.

When we were ten, we pinky swore we'd be best friends forever and when he held my hand I vowed to never let it go.

When we were twelve, the Pastor told us we could no longer whisper in the back pew. That we could no longer practice duets for service unless an adult was with us. That we could no longer roam the woods alone, guitars in hand, and sit in our spot by the edge of the creek, singing until the sun set.

His hair was light, and mine was dark. His eyes shone, and mine were heavy. They always were, even when I was a little girl. But where I was hard, he was soft, and where I wavered, he always believed. When my mother died, he wiped away my tears and told me to hold on to hope.

That all was not lost.

He kissed me when we were fourteen even though they told us it was sinful—for my lips were supposed to be saved for my husband alone—but he didn't care. Not about rules, at least.

He said he only cared about me.

I believed him.

His kiss was the sort of kiss I could write songs about. And I did. We were poor, our families always on the verge of losing it all. Not that we had much to lose. Electricity and hot water were never guarantees.

But there was one thing that could never be taken from me, even if there was no extra money.

No one could take the journal I hid under my pillow each night.

And I wrote pages and pages of lyrics on his lips alone. One single kiss, under the shade of an old oak tree, the branches swaying in the

September breeze, but my heart was sure and I wrote the song of my heart, binding it to my chest.

But when my father found the blasphemous words, he handed them to the Pastor, who burned them in front of all the other youths' eyes. We were the example, the dirty ones.

He told us to repent.

I cried.

He held my hand.

Everyone we grew up with in the church bore witness to this public humiliation.

He said he wasn't ashamed.

He said he loved me.

I told him I didn't love him back.

It was weak, I know—but I feared the wrath of my father. Of the pastor. Scared of them breaking me in ways that might never mend.

I can look back now and see that it was the final nail in the coffin, but back then we were still the Lord's Will Assembly, not the cult we became a few years later. He wasn't sent away— not then. Not yet. Instead, he was called a sinner like his older sister Harper. They made him make his wrongs right by constructing the church buildings. He would hammer nails into the wood until sweat dropped down his neck; until his hands bled.

It still wasn't enough.

The elders saw him as a marked man, though he was still a child.

I would see him working every time I entered the church... his eyes would find mine. And even though I was *just a girl,* I was no fool. I was a woman in enough ways. My body was alive, it had woken when he kissed me.

It would not go to sleep.

He loved me and I loved him and that should have been more than enough.

But it wasn't.

Because I was living in a world that was so small, so constricting, that I didn't know how to think on my own—how to stretch my wings, let alone soar.

Soon I was eighteen, and so was he. And he wanted me to run away with him, but I was scared.

"Let's go," he whispered, pleading with me. "Take my hand, and let me take you somewhere—"

I shook my head. I may have loved him, but we had no money, no car, and no education. My father told me daily where I would end up if I turned my back on God.

I may have been a woman... but I was a weak one.

He had been my lifeline when we were small

—problem was, I'd never learned to swim. And suddenly I was drowning, I didn't think I could make it to shore.

If I'd been stronger, my story would have ended up differently.

His would have too.

But I wasn't. And when he asked me to go, I was too scared to follow. So, he stayed too. Refusing to leave without me, even if it meant he was at the mercy of elders who thought of him as a sinner, and of themselves as saints.

For three years he watched and waited, making sure I was okay. Three years of never turning his back on me. In stolen conversations, he would tell me that I was his and he was mine and that he'd never leave. He was patient and he was relentless. The church changed my name from Abigail to Cherish, and I was more lost than ever about who I really was.

He got stronger each day with the back breaking work they asked him to do, his muscles stretching the seams of his ironed church clothes. His chiseled jaw and tanned skin became more dominating with each task they gave him.

As he grew strong, I grew fragile. Though I'd never admit that to him. I wanted him to believe I was as beautiful as I'd ever been. But I wasn't. So, I rarely left the house; I spent my days cooking and cleaning and helping home-school my younger siblings, since our mother died years ago, and I needed to be here for them. My hair got long and my bones grew weary. I didn't want him to see me then... see what had become of me.

I was ashamed. I didn't deserve his heart anymore. He deserved a woman who was brave enough to leave when he had asked.

I was older now. Old enough to be married.

And my father promised me to a man.

A man older than my father. A man who already had three wives.

A man who would pay my father ten thousand dollars to take me off his hands.

The family needed the money. I looked at the faces of my four younger siblings, hungry and longing for more than they had.

I had let him down, but I wouldn't fail my family too.

I agreed.

Tomorrow I would be bound to a husband who paid for me, my sole job to give him children.

The man I loved could let the dream of me go.

I wasn't enough for him anymore.

And deep down I wondered if I ever had been.

No, that isn't true. I didn't wonder.

I knew.

He deserved the world, and by marrying a stranger, I could give him a future bigger than the one he had here.

CHAPTER TWO

James

The sun beats down on my back, feeling like this godforsaken garage will never get done. I look over at Jonah wiping the sweat off his brow.

"I'm exhausted," he says. "Ready for lunch?"

I nod, and the two of us climb down the ladder.

"I'm ready to call it a day," I tell him. "It's hot as sin out here." It's barely noon and already it's ninety-five degrees. Idaho summers are no joke.

"What's going on over there?" Jonah asks, pointing to a group of women gathered around the entrance to the church.

I frown, not having heard about an event at the church today. Not that I care for the bullshit religion practiced at the compound—but still, I usually know what is happening and where seeing as I do most of the grunt work to set up different events.

I head to the communal kitchen in the back of the church and see my cousin Honor there, a baby on her hip, her free hand mixing coleslaw.

"Hungry, James?" she asks. Her eyes are lowered, and I wish she'd meet mine, but she's become withdrawn over the last few years, ever since she was forced to marry Luke, the head pastor of this congregation—which is a fancy way of saying brainwashed followers.

Though I sure as hell would never use a word like that.

"What's going on out front?" I ask, grabbing a ham sandwich from a platter on the counter. Jonah follows suit, and Honor pours us glasses of ice cold water.

"There's a wedding tomorrow. The sister-wives are getting the place ready."

I frown. "Whose wedding?"

Honor twists her lips, her voice small, nearly a whisper. "It's Cherish."

The white bread is caught in my throat, and I cough, trying to dislodge her words. How did I not know this was happening? The only reason I've stayed here for so long is to make sure Cherish is safe. All I can think at this moment is that I've failed her again.

Jonah whistles low beside me.

"I'm sorry, James," Honor says.

"I've gotta go find her."

"They won't let you get near her," Jonah says. "Not today."

But my heart is already racing. I've asked her, too many times to count, to come with me. To leave this life behind. But she's always refused.

Now there is no more time. Now she's getting fucking married.

I can't let this happen.

I refuse.

"I have to go try. I have to convince her—"

Honor nods. "You should go to her, James. Maybe she'll feel differently now that the reality is setting in." Honor looks up at me, tears in her pale blue eyes. "I know I would have left if given an out the night before my wedding."

I run a hand through my hair, jaw clenched, wondering how I can get through her father's front door without him pulling out his shotgun. That bastard hates me something fierce.

All because of a kiss.

A perfect, holy kiss.

A kiss I'll never forget. A kiss I received when I was just a boy; a kiss that made me a man.

I grab another sandwich, eating as I walk to

the door. Honor hands me a few cookies in a napkin. "Jonah, you'll cover for me?"

"Of course, man," he says. Jonah is a solid guy—though only eighteen. He's another part of the reason I can't just leave this place. I'm scared of what might happen to him when the elders try their damnedest to tear him down. Being here ensures I can help him stand up again.

But if I can get Cherish to leave with me, I'll go in a heartbeat. She *is* my heartbeat. My everything.

Has been ever since we were little.

I gave her my heart and never looked back.

Out on the dusty road outside the church, I try to think it through. If she's at home, it's gonna be hella hard to get to her. Still, I head in that direction. If she is getting married tomorrow, I literally have nothing to lose.

When I pass Elder Luke, I drop my head. He is in the middle of a conversation and doesn't notice me. His house is in the center of the compound, and Honor's sister-wives are on their front porch with a bunch of little ones. The farther out on the compound I go, I pass a row of trailers and know I am getting close to Cherish's father's place.

Before the church became so fundamental, we were all living in town, in our own places, but once Luke came back with a vision of the future, everyone moved to this plot of land that he owned. My father was an associate pastor, so he got set up pretty nice—thank God too because I have a bunch of younger siblings.

Cherish's dad, though, wasn't as lucky—though the truth is, he's always been down on his luck. There has never been enough money to go around for Cherish's family... and without a mother to help, the weight of the family has been on her shoulders.

When I get to their trailer, I see her younger brother Abe out front.

"What do you want?" he asks. He's only eight but already looks like he's seen better days.

"Is Cherish around?" I ask.

"Who wants to know?"

I pull back, not expecting this. Then again, I haven't been out here in a long time. Cherish turned me away so many times, I decided to wait her out for a while, not wanting to push her.

Now I wish I'd pushed her harder, faster. Stolen a van, taken all her siblings with me, got the hell out of this place.

"Just tell me where she is. Is she inside?"

He scowls, crossing his arms. A tougher sell than I expected.

I look down at my hands. "I'll give you a cookie."

He twists his lips. "Both of 'em," he barters.

I grin, liking his go-get-'em attitude. "Sure." I hand them over.

"She's at the creek. She's always at the creek when she's not here.

I nod in thanks, my chest constricting at the memories that well to the surface.

The creek.

Our creek.

Of course, she would be there.

I haven't been there in years.

"Thanks, little man," I tell him, already backing away from the trailer, snapping twigs as I run.

Needing to find her.

Needing to keep her.

Needing her to know she's always been mine.

CHAPTER THREE

Cherish

On the edge of the stream, I sit with my guitar propped under my arm, strumming the most familiar song I know. The one that I made my personal anthem a long time ago.

Before the church became so conservative, my family used to listen to music on an old record player my mom had from when she was a little girl. And she loved the Beach Boys.

I loved *If God Only Knows...* and I would sing that song, playing it on my guitar until my fingers were raw.

Now I sing it, my words barely audible because my face is streaked with tears.

I've been sitting out here for an hour, not wanting to be around anyone else right now. I don't think I could bear it.

So, I'm here alone, there's nothing here but

the creek that has always run with crystal clear water. Even before Pastor Luke brought us to this land, this was the spot I would come to with James. We've always lived within a mile of these woods.

I hear a branch snap, leaves rustle. Someone is here. I close my eyes, not wanting this moment to end.

"Abigail?"

I don't want James to see me here; to ask me why I didn't come find him first. I don't want him to see how fragile I feel, how undeserving I am. I didn't choose him because I was scared and I know how much I have hurt him.

He is here for me now.

Again.

Always.

I press my palm against the guitar strings, stopping them. I look over my shoulder and see him standing under an oak tree. Our oak tree.

His dark hair is pushed back from his forehead and he looks larger than ever, looming several feet above me. He looks like a real man, a man who could swoop in and protect me, a man I have denied. The only man I have ever wanted.

"James." My eyes sting with tears, and he rushes down to the river bank where I'm sitting on a fallen log.

"Abigail," he says again, now sitting beside me, lifting the guitar strap over my shoulder, setting the guitar behind us. He opens my palms and takes the guitar pick with a music note on the smooth surface, and he places it in his pocket. For safe keeping, he tells me.

"You're the only person who calls me that anymore," I tell him, missing the way my birth name sounds, but it also seems so foreign now, so removed. Not who I am, or at least who I have allowed myself to become.

He wraps his arm around me, knowing the cost of being caught. He doesn't care. For so long he has been careful, not doing anything that could compromise me. Avoiding long conversations with me—and recently any conversation at all. But now, under the shelter of the oak tree, with clear water running in the creek before us, it's like he is untethered from the compound rules a mile away. Out here in the woods, there are no rules, only us, and I remember what it was always like when we were young.

I wish it could always be this way.

"You can't get married tomorrow, Abigail. That can't be the way our story ends. We are supposed to be a love song."

I shake my head. "I don't even want you to look at me."

"Why?" he asks, squaring my shoulders to face him. Cradling my face in his hands. How many years have I longed for this moment? How long have I refused my heart what it wanted?

And for what? For a God who never heard the cries of my heart? My pleas and my prayers?

I want more than that.

I want James.

"I don't deserve you, James," I manage, closing my eyes, unable to look at him. Knowing his face is filled with nothing but devotion and not feeling like I deserve that sort of adoration. Not from a man like him.

"Shush, you don't need to cry. I'm here." He pulls my face to his. His lips are even better than I remembered. Soft and hard and here and now. Lips that press against mine and break something open. Wide open. My heart.

I sink into his kiss. His lips part, and so do mine, and he tips back my head, his arms around me, and I can feel how deeply he wants me. No, it's more than a want. It's a desire. A craving. A longing.

"I love you," he tells me between kisses, and then his tongue finds mine, and I whimper against him, his words a balm to my broken heart.

"I don't deserve this," I tell him. "I made you wait for so long."

"You were scared," he says, kissing me again. "Are you still scared?"

I shake my head, pulling away, wanting his kisses but also knowing the reality.

"George is paying my father ten thousand dollars for me. My brothers and sisters... they need me here. And that money can help them. I can't just—"

James shakes his head, refusing to hear it. "We can make a life and come back for them."

"They will never let me just go with you."

"We won't tell them." He kisses my fore-head. "I should have made you come with me a long time ago. Standing by only made you more scared. Scared of me. Of the idea of us."

"I'm not scared of you... I'm just scared of what you think of me, James." I pull back, covering my face with my hands.

"I think you are the only good thing in this place. The only good thing in this world. I love you, Abigail, and I'll cherish you forever. You chose not to go with me before, but when I heard that you were getting married, I knew in my heart I couldn't let this go on anymore. Let me be the man I was made to be. Let me take care of you."

"Do you have money?" I ask, knowing I have none.

He shakes his head. "I'll break into the

office, find some. I'll get us a car. We can go tonight when it's dark."

He speaks with fervor, passion, the same intensity he had three years ago. He hasn't wavered in his choice for a moment.

Why am I so weak when all I want is to be strong?

"Say yes." He cups my face again, our eyes locked on one another. My body knows exactly what it wants, even though it feels reckless and dangerous. The men on the compound have guns and are vengeful. They don't let people leave without their permission. If we got caught I'd never be able to help my siblings.

But if we don't try what sort of life will they have?

"Do you love me?" he asks.

"Do you have to ask?" I bite my bottom lip, not believing he's really here, holding my face and choosing me. Still.

"No," he says. "I know you've always loved me. The same way I've always loved you. Love is enough."

Part of me wonders if that kind of thinking is naive: to believe love will solve all our problems... but I want to believe in that sort of power right now. What else do I have?

An old man who will force me into his bed, have his way with me.

I don't want that.

I want James.

"Come with me," he says. "Please."

I lift my chin, looking at the face I memo-rized as a four-year-old, the face I have always known was mine.

"Where you go, I will follow," I tell him. "But first, kiss me again."

CHAPTER FOUR

James

She says yes, and as she does, it's as if nearly a decade's worth of weight has fallen from her shoulders. I wrap my arms around her, unable to restrain myself from deepening our kiss, our embrace. Her hands are on my chest, tugging at my shirt.

I want her more than she knows, but I will let the woman I've always loved take the lead. I don't want to push her when she's vulnerable, but I also know the love we have has blossomed over a lifetime, and damn, we've bided our time.

"I want you in ways you don't know," I growl in her ear. Her hunger is real as she kisses my neck, exploring more of me, returning to my lips and kissing them hard. Abigail may be a fragile flower, but she's more than that.

The Abigail I fell in love with knew passion,

knew the language of love because it was written on her heart strings and then plucked from her guitar every time she picked up her instrument.

"James," she whispers. "I think I know how you want me. And I want you that way too."

She pulls back, meeting my gaze with a sure nod. "When you kissed me when we were fourteen, my body woke up to you... it has never gone back to sleep."

My cock twitches, damn those words are sweet and forbidden and luscious and ours. "All this time you wanted me pressed against you?"

She shakes her head ever so softly. "No, I wanted you pressed *inside* of me."

"Oh, love," I groan, wanting to strip her here and now, take her under our oak tree, and in the shallow creek, I want to kiss her breasts, see them in all their glory, trace our love on her skin and fill her up and make her whole.

"We've waited long enough," she tells me, unbuttoning her blouse. "I want to ask for your forgiveness, for making you wait so long. I want my body to be an offering, to you." Her blouse drops from her shoulders, revealing creamy skin and a simple white bra covering her breasts.

"Don't say things like that, you have nothing to apologize for. This life of ours, it isn't normal.

It's fucked us up in ways we might never understand."

"I've hurt you, though, and I'm sorry." She reaches back and unclasps her bra. She drops it next to her blouse. Her tits are full and big, made for loving. "And I know we can't go back in time, but I can give you what I've always wanted you to have. All of me. So, take it. Take me now."

It's all I need to hear. I've been saving my body for her because it's always been about her. And now I will give her what we both so badly want.

I run my hands over her breasts, two big luscious globes that get me all bothered under the hot sun and blue sky. My cock grows thick as my fingers run over her beautiful nipples, hard under my fingertips. I have dreamt of this moment for most of my life: her in my arms, offering herself to me. It's more than I can goddamn take.

Growling, I tear off my t-shirt, take her blouse, and lay them together on the leafy ground for a makeshift blanket. The soil is soft, and I need her on her back. I need to see all of her at once, then I'll pull her to me and worship her body like the gift it is.

She licks her lips, sitting on this tree trunk, without her top on, and with the covering of the trees, and the burbling creek, it's as if we're protected from the rest of the world in this wooded oasis of our own making.

"I haven't seen you without a shirt since you became... became..." She licks her lips again.

I step toward her, her knees parting, and I stand between them, looking down at this woman I've known for forever. "Became what, Abigail?"

She hooks her thumbs through the belt loops on my blue jeans, her chest heaving in anticipation. "Since you became a man."

She looks up at me then gingerly reaches up, touches my abs, running her hands over the ladder of muscles. I've worked outside for years, staying here so I could make sure she was safe, and all that work has put my body in peak condition. I'm glad she likes what she sees because I goddamn love my view of her.

"Your body is a piece of artwork," she says, biting the corner of her lip in disbelief.

"No, you are the piece of art. I want to see all of you."

She nods but doesn't make a move to stand and take off her skirt. Instead, she unbuttons my jeans, tugs them down, and my cock is begging to be released. Her warm hands are so close to my thick manhood, and it's throbbing with desire, having waited so damn long for this moment. I've released myself over the years thinking of her creamy skin, of her curvy body atop mine, her pussy filled with my length. I've imagined it, gotten off to it—but this is no daydream. No fantasy. No, this is real.

She pushes down my boxers, and when she does, her chest heaves, her mouth parts, her lips are licked, her eyes flutter.

"James, you are so..."

"You can't keep holding back your thoughts, love. What happened to the girl who could tell me anything? Who knew her secrets were safe with me?"

She opens her eyes wide, swallows. "I'm still here."

I run my finger over her soft cheekbone, lifting her chin. "Tell me what you see."

"I see your cock, so big, so hard." Her face flushes at the dirty words, words that I'm guessing she's never uttered, words I'm surprised she even knows. But before the church went fundamental, we'd go to the mall, watch movies, read books. She may have been sheltered, but even as teenagers, we still had access to the outside world.

"And do you like what you see?" I ask.

She sighs, her shoulder relaxing. "James, I love what I see."

"What does it do to you, when you see my big cock, nice and hard for you?"

"It makes me wet... down there." She lowers her gaze, and I know she's talking about her sweet pussy.

"How wet?" I ask, inching my cock closer to her. I stroke myself and my long cock gets harder still.

"So wet, wetter than I usually get when I think about you."

I groan, stroking myself more, wanting her to touch me, but not wanting to push her. "You think about me?"

She laughs softly, reaching for my length, wrapping her hand around me, and running her fingers over my length, cupping my balls, pre-come releasing at my tip with her gentle touch.

"So many times, James, that I think I've worn out my prayer bench kneeling and repenting."

"But you aren't going to repent for this, are you?"

She shakes her head, her eyes welling up with emotion. "No, no more apologies. I think I'm just realizing how much time I wasted being scared. Missing out on what I wanted because of it."

"I don't want my love to be scared."

"I'm not scared now, but like I said," she

says, smiling through her tears, "I *am* wet. And I want you to see what you do to me."

I raise a brow, my cock at attention, and I know I'm going to fucking explode in her pussy the moment she spreads her legs.

She must understand, and when she dips her head, widening her mouth, licking the come from my tip, my lifelong fantasies come to fruition. Abigail is sucking my cock in the same place we shared our first kiss. She moves her head, her mouth tight around my length. She looks up at me, her eyes filled with pleasure, her mouth filled with my manhood, and she looks so fucking hot—her tits bouncing, her head bobbing and her hands all over me. I know I'm gonna come hard and fast.

"Oh, love," I tell her, knowing I'm close. She must sense this because she moves faster, and I know she must be gagging; no way can she take all of me in her mouth, but she keeps sucking with her lips suctioned around my stiffness. I come in her, hard, and her hands are on my ass, pulling me against her mouth, like she wants more, needs more, demands all of me.

My come shoots into her warm mouth, and she moans, swallowing me, sucking me still, as if she wants every last salty taste of me.

I'll give her what she wants.

Now and forever.

CHAPTER FIVE

Cherish

I swallow what he gives me, and I don't care if the church condemns me—right now what I just shared with James is the holiest exchange of love in this world.

But then he lowers me to my back, slips off my skirt, then my panties, bringing the wet pair to his nose, inhaling my womanhood, and I know I've yet to experience the holiest of holy.

"Oh, love," James says, running his hand over my skin, parting my knees, touching me as if I'm the most precious thing he's ever touched. "Your pussy is perfection."

I smile, not embarrassed or ashamed—my best friend is looking at me, loving everything he sees, and it makes me whimper under his hand. As he touches me, I see his cock growing large again, and my belly is already full of his baby gravy, but I want more.

"You like it?" I ask, marveling at the fact that James is going to be my first. I've dreamt of this, but never actually imagined it for myself. Why should I get what I want after holding back for so long? But James doesn't seem angry at me for holding back from him for so long, he is patient in ways I don't understand. James came and found me before it was too late, and now we can be together—come what may.

"Your pussy is untouched, so nice and tight. Your pussy was made for my cock, love, you know that, right?"

I smile again, trying to reconcile the way I view myself with the way James sees me now. I spread my legs wider for him, wanting him to take all I have to offer.

"I died and went to heaven, love," he tells me, his hand stroking my slit, and when he touches me, my entire body shivers with antici- pation, my heart flutters, and my bottom lifts, as if gravitating toward the place his hand is, wanting him to be closer, wanting him inside me.

"Don't make me wait, James," I say, wrap- ping my arms around his neck, drawing him to me. My legs wrap around him, and when he inches himself into me, I call out in pleasure.

My body is starved for attention, and his body is the only thing to satisfy my cravings. Cravings I didn't even know were mine for the taking.

He pushes in me, and I wince as he fills me up, pressing past the place that has made me a virgin. "Am I hurting you?" he asks, his elbows on either side of me.

I shake my head imperceptibly. "No, it's okay, I don't want you to stop," I moan, meaning it. It hurts, but not in a painful way, in a searing, my body is filled perfectly, never let me go way. A way I need. A way I want.

A way that is ours.

He is in me now, and his lips are on mine. He kisses me as he makes love to me. This man that I've wanted forever has come and claimed me. And we don't know what tomorrow will bring, but that is going to be okay. As he rocks inside of me, my pussy throbs, my clit is exposed and greedy, rubbing against him and taking all the pleasure offered.

My body is alive, and when he thrusts deeper into me, my legs shake, my thighs tremble, and I come. I come against and for him and with him. He comes in me too, filling me with his creamy release, the release made for me. The release we share.

I want it again and again and I want it forever.

I will have it.

But before he even stops rocking against me, before my body steadies itself, soaking up all he gave me, we hear a rustle in the trees. Branches snapping.

We stop moving, hearing the footsteps, the hollers, the calls.

Someone is looking for me.

Several someones are looking for me.

"Cherish, where are you, woman?"

James locks eyes with me. Wordlessly, we move quickly, pulling on pants and buttoning shirts and sliding on shoes, and the people are moving faster through the thicket.

And then they are here, a group of men, my father and husband to be, Luke too, and James's father. Everyone looks at him, then me, anger on their faces, fear in my heart. But I am dressed and James is dressed and there is nothing to prove.

But that doesn't matter. Not to these men. Men who are motivated by a God I don't understand, a God who has forsaken me and left me more times than I can count.

"What in God's name is going on out here?" my father yells.

George, the man I am meant to marry, moves closer to me as if sniffing the air. He asks the question that would put James in the grave if he chose to be honest.

"You tarnishing my bride to be?" he yells.

James is steel-faced and jaw clenched and he moves to step in front of me. I will him not to, knowing my father like I do, knowing through the grapevine of women how they are treated by their husbands. The men here put on a good show, some may not even physically hurt their wives, but emotional abuse is real too, and I am terrified of the affliction.

Not just to me, but the way they may hurt James.

But he doesn't care. He only has eyes for me.

He looks at me, his heart raw and mine for the taking. I will take it, now and for always, but I can't bear to see him hurt.

But he loves me. He always has and he tells them that.

"Cherish is the woman I love, the woman I want to marry. You can't come between us."

I love him for his bravery, for his honor, and his commitment.

But as a shovel is raised by the hands of a man I don't even know, and is slammed across the back of James' head, I know he is also a fool.

Because he may love me, but his words will cost him everything.

I was right for never giving in before, I knew what our love would cost him.

His life.

They swing the shovel again, and he falls backward into the shallow creek. His head is bloody, the clear water turning dark as he's pushed under the current. Once, twice.

I try to run toward him, but I'm dragged away, my screams loud, until I force them to stop. I muffle them with my knuckles, knowing every cry for mercy will result in more pain for my beloved. I turn my head, watching as he is beaten to a pulp.

Watching as the man I love is murdered by my father, my family.

No.

No.

No.

I stop screaming, not knowing how to use my voice once James is gone. I start pulling away from the hold I'm in, bound by my father and George. I fall to the wooded ground, my body desperate to crawl backward, toward him.

Toward James.

But they won't let me. They pull me to standing, dragging me away from the river, away from the man I love.

In the distance, he makes no cries, no pleas, nothing.

I'm taken from the oak tree and led away to a life I never wanted but had been too scared to break free from.

I'm led away from James.

And in my heart, I know I am the very thing that killed him.

After all, if he had never met me, he'd still be here.

Instead, he's gone forever.

CHAPTER SIX

James

Over the last year, I've been through hell and back.

But I'm still standing.

Still breathing.

Still holding onto hope.

Cherish.

Cherish.

Cherish.

She may have grown up as Abigail, but now... now her name is exactly right. I cherish her in all the ways that matter. Her name is always on my lips. On my mind. A part of my soul.

I live for her, though it's been a full year since I laid her perfect body on the bed of the forest, under the hot sun and blue sky. A year since I saw her smile in a way I hadn't seen in years. She was vulnerable and broken, but in my arms, she felt whole.

I saw that in her eyes when she looked at me, asking for forgiveness she never needed. She is my salvation, and I don't need her to be a martyr, dying for an idea about herself that was never true.

At least never true for me.

But it's been a year and a lot can happen in twelve months' time.

God knows I've seen it all.

Like waking up beaten and half-dead on a freight train headed south. I would have jumped, but my arm was broken, along with some ribs and a busted ankle—that much was clear. My head was cloudy, my memory shot; I didn't know if I was a day from Idaho or five. And when I finally came to and stepped off the train when it came to a stop, I found I wasn't alone. Jonah was with me, making me drink water, trying his hardest to clean my bandages. He kept me alive.

"What happened?" I asked, willing myself to stand, palm trees around us, salty air working to wash away the blood and broken bones.

Jonah looked at me, then hanging his head, he tells me it was his fault. Someone noticed I was gone, asked where I'd gone. His excuse didn't add up, and they beat the shit out of him, holding nothing back. Apparently, word had gotten out that my interest in Cherish had never waned, after all these years. And George wanted me gone before his wedding, not trusting a young bastard like me around his woman.

When Jonah recounted the day, I gritted my teeth, wanting to punch someone or something. They'd beat the shit out of both of us, left us for dead, but then they put us on a freight train, not wanting our murders on their holy hands.

I'd be dead if Jonah had taken as bad a beating as I had.

But we were broke and had nowhere to go. Too terrified to go back where we came from—knowing our skulls would be smashed right through, were we to ever return.

I yelled to the sky, demanding justice. Begged for a sign. I reached in my pants pocket, not finding any dollar bills, but my fingers found Cherish's guitar pick.

It is the only sign I ever needed.

Her.

Mine.

"What now?" Jonah asked.

"Now we make a plan to get back to where we belong."

Jonah shook his head. "No way in hell. I wanted out, but was scared to run in case they decided to find me. Now I'm free, no way am I ever going back there."

I nodded, understanding. I wasn't going back there to stay.

I'd only return once.

To get what was mine all along.

And a year later I'm ready. The time is now.

Jonah is older, and of course, we all are, but he was 18 when we left the compound, and in that time, he's grown into his skin. He's taller, stronger, ready to take life by the horns.

I'm glad because when I leave here, I'm not coming back. But Jonah is gonna be okay here on his own.

We've worked hard this past year, scraping by, living on the street until I got cleaned up enough that the two of us could stay at a homeless shelter. Thankfully the freight train stopped in Miami, and so roughing it isn't as hard as it might have been in, say, Boston. We got through the winter without starving, so that's something.

Eventually, we started working construction jobs, it took some convincing to get hired on sites without any references, but once we had a tool in hand, our work spoke for itself.

We made enough to get an apartment and work is steady now that we have a solid place on a crew. But I keep socking all my money away, knowing that when I return to Idaho, I'm gonna need enough money to start a life with Cherish.

Knowing it might be hard to get her out, but I'm not stopping until my woman is in my arms.

At the bus station, Jonah claps me open my back. "Feel good to ride back in a Greyhound instead of the way we came down here?"

"Damn straight." I pull Jonah into an embrace. I owe him my life. He and I have fought to stand on our own two feet, and I know that we're never going back to where we came from. "You keep your chin up, Jonah, you hear me?"

"You sound older than a twenty-four-year-old, fucker, you know that, right?" he asks.

I pull back, grinning at the mouth on this kid. A year in the real world hardened us up real damn fast: if we weren't real men before, we sure as fuck are now.

"I expect to hear from you, understand?" I raise a brow at him, trying to remain stoic, but inside I'm fucking torn up. Saying goodbye to Jonah is saying goodbye to family.

"Yeah, I'll text you," he tells me. "And you better let me know where you are, all right?"

"Don't go doing something stupid, you

hear?" I tell him, waving goodbye as I board the bus, duffel bag slung over my shoulder.

"Go get your woman," he hollers as I walk down the aisle to my seat.

I cock my head out the half-opened window, and shout, "I love ya, bro."

He raises his chin, salutes me, and the bus pulls out.

I'm gonna go get my woman all right.

And I'm not letting anything keep me from her again.

CHAPTER SEVEN

Cherish

The whisperings grow to a roar and I know what I need to do.

What I should have done a long time ago.

After James died and Honor left—leaving a scandal in her wake—police officers began knocking on doors. CPS reports were filed and everyone at the compound knew we needed to leave.

The men were the only ones who knew where we were going.

But I know I can't go with them.

As my sister-wives help George prepare for our new start—canning vegetables, packing trucks with tools and equipment—I prepare for my own departure.

There's a twelve-passenger van that I keep

loading with dry goods, and extra pots or pans, linens, and of course all the baby gear.

Because it isn't just me leaving. My triplets, who are three months old, are coming with me.

This year has changed my life ... and that is the understatement of the century.

I fill up milk jugs with water and stow them in the van, with bars of soap and toothpaste. I take a little of everything as discreetly as possible. Thankfully, everyone is so preoccupied with leaving that they don't realize what I am doing.

A year ago, Honor left, and then her sister-wives True and Kind followed. If they are brave enough to go, I can be brave too.

And I know where I'm headed. A place James's family took me to once when we were kids. High up in the Idaho Mountains, James's uncle had an old cabin that was abandoned. A bunch of families from the church would go up there for picnics, and all of us kids played hide and go seek for hours. I remember shrieking with laughter, running through a field filled long grass, then going deep in the forest where there were trees with trunks wider than I could reach around.

The cabin was abandoned then, and I'm hoping it still is. It's not like I have any money —aside from enough for a single tank of gas. It must work. Word has gotten out that Honor and Harper live up there in the same mountains, but that their husbands built them fancy homes. I hope the run-down cabin hasn't been torn down... and I'm holding onto the little bit of faith I have left in this world that it's still standing.

I'm standing in the kitchen when George comes in. His eyes brighten when he sees Andrew in my arms.

"How's my son today?" he asks. I swallow at his words, knowing Andrew is no more his son than I am his wife. He may have taken me in his bed, but I had already given my heart, body, and soul to another. I may live here with George—but he is nothing to me. He is worse than nothing. He watched James's murder, and in all this time has never mentioned it. James's death and the disappearance of Jonah are unspoken history.

But it isn't dead to me. The memory of James is alive and well. And every time I look at our children, Harmony, Jacob, and Andrew, I know James lives on through them.

That is why I must take this opportunity now that I have it. I was too scared to leave while pregnant—the pregnancy required me to be on bedrest for months—but now they are here, healthy and growing, and I can take them from this place that destroyed their father.

"He's well, husband," I say, addressing George in the only way I am allowed. "And, how are you?"

George looks at me greedily. "I will be better once I take you to bed."

My stomach churns. I've avoided sleeping with George for a long time, but I know if I stay here, he will require me to lie with him again.

Which is just one more reason I must go.

"As you wish, just as soon as the midwife clears me I will join you in our marriage bed."

I look up at him, forcing a small smile on my face, knowing I have to play the part for the rest of the day.

Because I'm leaving tonight.

And never coming back.

"Good, good, Cherish." He leans in close, his coffee breath pungent and his pot-belly forcing me to pull away. But he won't let me. He holds my chin, drawing himself closer to me. "Because you are my favorite wife. The youngest and most fertile. There is nothing that will ever stop me from taking your body again."

"What is mine is yours," I tell him in a whisper.

"When we start our new life, you must know I am going to give you everything you desire."

I bite my lip. "And where will our new life be? Where is this promised paradise?"

George smirks. "You want answers?"

I smile coyly. "Everyone is talking about Wyoming. Is that where we are moving this week?"

George shakes his head. "I'll tell you, but only after you've given me a kiss."

Andrew starts crying in my arms, and I am grateful for the disturbance. It breaks the spell George is under and allows me to leave the kitchen quickly. "Sorry, he needs a diaper change."

George nods, pursed lips, that hungry look still in his eye. He reaches for my bottom, squeezing it tight. "It's Montana, and tonight, I need you in my room. Midwife's orders or not. I demand it."

I flash him a smile as I leave the room with Andrew, who's now sobbing. He must have been as uncomfortable in the presence of George as I was.

I need to go.

Now.

I originally planned to leave when the sky was inky black and the house quiet, but after seeing George in the kitchen, I can't risk him looking for me in the middle of the night. And if I take the babies when everyone is asleep, what happens if one of them cries and wakes people up?

The sister-wives hate me, mostly because I birthed triplets nine months after my wedding day. And the fact that two of them were boys, and all of them were healthy, made me the envy of the older wives. But they can have all of George's attention—I never wanted any of it.

So, when I see them in the kitchen cleaning up the mess from dinner, I try to make an excuse as to why I'm leaving right after supper. With the babies.

"I am going down to see the midwife," I tell them.

"At this hour?" Treasure looks at the clock on the microwave. "It's after 6 o'clock."

I nod. "I know... but George requested me tonight... And I need her to make sure I'm okay... to lie with him."

They all know the birth was brutal, and that my body was battered afterward. The babies are just twelve weeks old now, and it isn't unreasonable that I have put off being with George. But they know he's moody about having had to wait so long to have me. I'm sure they realize the whole house will be happier if George can sleep with me again.

Not as if that's actually going to happen...
but they don't know that.

"And I thought, while I am down there, she
can check on the babies, make sure they are
okay."

"Why wouldn't they be?" Treasure asks.

I shrug. "I think Jacob has a cold."

"In July?"

"I know, strange, isn't it?" I smile serenely as
if I'm as confused as she is.

"Do you need someone to accompany you?"

"No, I'm fine. I'll take the old van. Everyone
hates that thing, but I don't mind it."

Four of Treasure's daughters are here now,
helping with dishes, and she's distracted—
exactly what I hoped would happen.

I walk past them and put the babies in a
sling. Harmony on one side, Jacob slung across
the other shoulder, and Andrew in an infant car
seat. It's cumbersome, but I only need to get to
the van. The front door is wide open, and
everyone is distracted. Older boys are packing
boxes for our move and there are children
playing in the front yard.

I move quickly, deliberately. James would
have wanted me to go. His death opened my
eyes to the world in which I live.

I will escape, remembering the father of my

children with every mile I put between them and this horror-house I've called home.

And then in a flash, I've buckled up the children, put the key in the ignition, and I drive out under the guise of visiting the midwife who lives on the other side of the compound.

This is going to work. It has to.

I've already lost James.

I can't bear to lose anything more. And not just for me.

For my babies, too.

James wanted to rescue me all along, and I hope somehow, somewhere, he knows that he has.

CHAPTER EIGHT

James

When I get to town, I start asking questions.

But there isn't a lot in the way of answers.

The people at the compound left over a week ago, in the dead of the night.

At the gas station store, I press. "What do you mean they all just disappeared? Surely there has got to be more detail than that?"

The clerk just shakes his head. "Sorry, son. You know those people?"

"I used to." I feel a dark pain sear through my heart. "Are the cops involved?"

The clerk frowns. "Word is they have no reason to be. Guess CPS had been poking their noses around after that woman left, caused a bit of a scandal, but nothing came of it."

My eyes narrow. "A woman left?"

The clerk shrugs, raising his hands in the air.

"I don't know much, I just hear things. A woman left, pressed charges of abuse against the leader, says she was a sister-wife or something? Not sure about all that besides the HBO show Big Love. If there was polygamy, the cops would have cracked down harder, I'd have thought."

I laugh sharply. "Oh, there was polygamy all right."

"Sorry, I can't help you."

I nod, understanding. With my bag over my shoulder, I walk the two miles to the compound. It's a warm day, and I'm reminded of the last time I say Cherish.

It's hard to accept that she isn't here now, but I figured it might be a long road to travel before she was back in my arms.

I'm not giving up hope.

Not now, not ever.

When I get to the property a fuckton of memories floods me, fast. I don't remember leaving this place, was passed out when they run Jonah and me away, but I sure remember being here. The dusty gravel road, the piles of tires. The buildings Jonah and I built one by one.

But the clerk at the gas station was right. This place has become a ghost town. After walking around for an hour, looking at Cherish's dad's old trailer—ransacked and empty— I'm done.

I find an abandoned car and can hot wire it. But thankfully, once I sit and buckle up, I find a key ring deep in the door pocket. I wouldn't say my luck has turned around, but at least I have a car to get me out of here.

There's only one place I can think of to go... my sister's house. Trouble is, it's a place I've never actually been to before. But, it's the only place I can think of where I might be able to find some answers.

I don't know Harper's address, but I do know she's living in the Idaho State Forest. I was there when I was younger. My uncle, who has long since passed, had an old place up there and we'd go there when we were kids. My dad would fish and we kids would roam the property. Life was sure different before everyone got wrapped up in Luke's cult.

There's only one small street at the base of the mountain, so far as Google Maps is concerned. I drive there and find a motel for the night. It isn't nice, but I've certainly seen worse.

I wouldn't say I sleep soundly, in fact, night-mares—like not knowing what has happened to Cherish—mess with my mind. When the sun rises, I'm relieved. I can't bear another night without answers.

The only diner in town is open and a woman named Rosie serves me coffee and scrambled eggs.

"And where are you traveling from?" she asks, hands on her hips as if it's her business to know every person's business who walks in here.

Figuring she may actually be the first step in finding my sister, I tell her the truth. "I'm looking for a woman named Harper, she's my sister."

Rosie about near drops her coffee pot. "You're James?"

Shocked that she knows who I am, I ask the obvious question. "Where is she?"

She sits down in the booth, opposite me. "She's not far. Up the mountain, less than a half-hour away."

"Can I get directions?" I wipe my mouth, already standing from the booth.

———

Twenty minutes later I'm pulling up to a

gorgeous cabin. I whistle low, amazed at this custom home.

Before the shitty car is in park, Harper's already running toward me with arms wide open.

"James," she says, her eyes filled with tears, she wraps me in a huge bear hug and doesn't let go. "You're so big. So tall. And you have a beard. You're all grown up!"

The thing is, Harper and I are just a few years apart, but the older we got, the farther apart we grew. Her warm embrace is more than I expected, but it isn't until she is hugging me that I realize how hard it's been to not have anyone in my corner this past year. Jonah and I were lone rangers, doing the best we could to scrape by, and I never had time to dwell on the past—I only imagined my future with Cherish.

When she pulls back we take a good look at one another. She's all grown up. She's a twenty-six-year-old wife and mother. Behind her, on the porch, are her triplets and little girl. They're watching us intently, and then the boys start asking who I am, and what I'm here for.

"This is your Uncle James," Harper says. "My brother."

"You have a bro-bro?" a little guy asks.

I smile, kneeling before him. "Yeah, I'm your mama's little brother."

"Why have we never met you?" another boy asks.

At this, I look up at Harper who's wiping her eyes. "Because, Cedar, sometimes life makes it hard to see the people you love."

"Did you miss him?" he asks his mama.

"Very much."

At this, her little ones beam. "Party?" the little girl asks. "Tea party, mama!?"

Harper laughs, picking up the little girl. "No tea party now. Later. Let mama have a cup of coffee with her brother first, okay?"

They listen, running into the house, and Harper and I follow behind them.

"Your home is beautiful," I tell her, noticing the custom woodwork, the fine banister, and built-in bookcases, the fireplace is massive, covered in river rock and is a focal point for the room.

The other place your eyes can't help but land on is the wall of family photos. There are dozens of frames: the kids sitting under a Christmas tree, fishing with their dad, photos of Harper and Jaxon on a TV set—the logo for a reality show behind them, and what looks like a big vacation with friends at a lake. Looking at them, I feel pride in my sister, for carving herself such a beautiful and rich life.

That is what I want with Cherish.

That is what I'm determined to find.

Harper calls to me from the kitchen, but before I turn to answer, my eyes land on another photograph of a family that isn't my sisters. The man's arms are covered in tattoos, and he's holding newborn twins. Next to him are three more children, stair-stepped in age, looking about 3, 2, and 1. And with them is a woman I know. Well.

"Is that Honor?" I ask, choking on my words. Honor. As in Luke's Honor. As in, what the actual hell.

Then Cedar is back, standing beside me. "Yeah, that's Auntie Honor. And that's Uncle Hawk. You're my uncle, too. You should be best friends."

I walk into the kitchen with wide eyes. "Auntie Honor?" I shake my head, pulling up on a stool at the island. "What is going on here? Have you been to the compound? Where are mom and dad? The rest of our siblings?"

Harper pulls her lips together tight, pouring us coffee, and pausing a beat too long.

"It's a long story."

"I have nowhere to be." I take the coffee and lift it to my lips. "And I've got a story of my own."

"You go first," Harper says. "Where in God's name have you been?"

She tells me all about Honor running away—just
weeks after I left— and then meeting Jaxon's
cousin Hawk, falling love, and having his twins,
just a few months ago.

And I explain what happened the night
Abigail's father and his buddies knocked me out
and left me for dead on a freight train. By then
I've finished two cups of coffee and am tired of
talking.

"I can't believe they did that to you. I bet
Abigail thinks you're dead if she saw all that."
Harper wipes a tear from her eye. "Well, I can
believe it, I'm just so sorry. And Jonah is in Flor-
ida, all alone?"

"He had no reason to return. His family is as
fucked up as ours, only he didn't have a woman
to come back for."

"And you do?"

I look at her like she's crazy. "I've gotta find
Cherish."

"Cherish?" Harper scrunches up her nose.

"Abigail."

Harper's face falls. "I wish I had an answer
for you. After Honor and her sister-wives left,
there was reportedly some police activity at the
compound. No one left for a while, several
months passed, but then the police cases were

closed, and the compound had made right for whatever shady activity was going on."

"Then why did they go?" I ask.

Harper shrugs. "We have no idea, James. We only know they're gone at all because it was in the paper. No one up on the mountain has any contact with the Lord's Will Church... and we want to keep it that way. I have nothing against believing in God, or a higher power... but we have major issues with brainwashing women and children, and denying women rights to their bodies."

"Believe me, Harper, I'm on your side here. I don't want to see dad ever again; he was there when I was beaten with a shovel." I feel the anger rising within me, and I wish with all that I am that I could erase history, make the past disappear.

"They must have kept it real quiet. Honor thought you had run away or they ran you out. No one knew you were beaten and forced away like that."

I run a hand over my beard. "I know you want nothing to do with that cult, but I have to find it. Find her. Cherish is with them, and she is my everything, Harper."

She presses her hand to her chest. "I just don't want you finding them... they will kill you."

I see she's broken up about what they did to me—and I understand—but what she doesn't realize is that I would do anything to get Cherish back.

"I don't have a choice, dammit. I love her."

At this Harper nods. "I'm just scared you're going to get hurt... and what if—"

I shake my head, ending the conversation. "There are no *what-if*s when it comes to Cherish and me. I've loved her since I was four years old."

Harper bit her bottom lip, but neither of us says anymore. The truth is, she and I both know we have no idea where the cult went.

And I could be spending a long-ass time looking down dead ends to find her.

Later that night, once we've finished dinner, Jaxon and I are on the front porch having a beer, and looking out at his gorgeous piece of property. The sky is still blue, the days in July stretching nice and long, and the kids are outside on the playground their father built them.

Jaxon's a big burly guy, but I'm damn burly myself. Working construction in Miami has taken away all my soft edges and made my exterior hard in ways it never used to be.

"Look," Jaxon says. "We can always use a hand on our crew. I heard you've worked construction for years—you'd be an asset to us. You can stay here for a while until—"

"No, Jaxon, you don't get it." I set down my beer. "I know you and Harper think I'm headed off on a wild goose chase but—"

Jaxon cuts me off. "Hell no, you wanna find your woman? Good. I want that for you too. I don't want her living with those motherfuckers. I want you to be happy. All I'm saying is, once you find her, what's your plan? Maybe get yourself a fucking house, a place your woman can make a home. Otherwise, it's gonna be damn hard to—"

Now it's my turn to cut him off. "I get it, Jaxon, I do. It's complicated and I need a plan. I realize—even if I do find where they've relocated—I can't just show up and demand she come with me. They almost killed me for being alone with her." I sigh, shaking my head. "But that doesn't mean I'm going to stop trying."

I've said my piece, and surprisingly it doesn't get me any pushback from Jaxon. Maybe he respects me for drawing a line in the sand.

"Look," I tell him. "I've been traveling for

weeks. I'm exhausted and just need some space clear my head." Looking at all the kids fussing now over Harper's bedtime call, I know I need more peace and quiet than this house tonight. "I'm thinking of heading up to my uncle's old cabin and checking it out. Stay there for the night to just decompress. You been out there lately?"

Jaxon shakes his head. "Not in the last year or so. We thought about trying to buy the land from your father—the deed's in his name—but we didn't want to mess with him."

"I can understand that." Running my hand over my neck, I ask, "Do you have a sleeping bag I can borrow, maybe a few granolas bars or something to tide me over?"

Jaxon nods. "I can set you up with gear all right. I'll even throw in a bottle of whiskey. I'm thinking you could use a stiff drink or two."

CHAPTER NINE

Cherish

I've been up here a month. No one has come looking for me, thank God.

I'm cut off from the outside world, but I don't mind. In fact, I'm glad. I don't want to know what happened to everyone when they left the compound. Or if they left at all.

Knowing that kind of information is only going to stress me out and hold me back. Right now, I can't have that. Right now, I need to focus on my babies. On our survival.

Our future.

The cabin is in rough shape, but what's new? I'm in rough shape myself. But honestly, this place could be infested with rodents and I wouldn't mind. I'm experiencing the sweet taste of freedom for the first time in my life, and it's more beautiful than I could've ever imagined.

We drove up here when it was late at night, and spent the first night in the van. I'd nurse one baby, buckle them back in their car seat, and then nurse the next. I rotated like that for hours, and eventually, they all passed out with milk drool on their chin. Then I could capture a few hours of rest myself.

The next day I got to work. On the lush, green grass I laid out a blanket and set my babies in a row while I began unloading my van. I wasn't intimidated by the undertaking—I was motivated by it.

I may be sheltered and naïve in some ways, and surely my education is lacking—but my common sense? It's at full throttle. After losing James, I stopped being so scared. Not outwardly, of course, I still maintained a meek and mild demeanor, and in a lot of ways, I didn't even have a choice in it. I was on bedrest for months.

But inwardly, the way I thought about things really began to change. I worked to forgive myself for having been scared for so long, not accepting the love that James had been offering me so freely.

I regret that I hadn't been able to. With all that I am, I regret that. He gave me a gift he'll never know he gave. His death opened my heart and mind. I wanted to be a braver and stronger mother for my children. I wanted to be the kind of woman James would be proud of. That is why I planned this exit. That's why I'm here right now, digging up dirt in a tidy row, planting lettuce and spinach. That's why I am at this cabin, creating a makeshift home, with no intention of leaving—because I am stronger now.

Eventually, someone will find me. I just have this sinking feeling, but it's not gonna happen for a while. Also, I can't sit around fearing what will happen next. I'm choosing to live today to its fullest capacity. I'm choosing to kneel before a patch of earth and plant tiny seeds, knowing that whatever pokes out of the ground will be food that will nourish me.

Inside the cabin, I hear a baby crying. There are bassinets in the one room cabin, and I stand, wiping my hands on my long cotton nightgown, it's much too hot for the heavy clothes I wore back at the compound. Taking my trowel with me, I set it on the front porch, along with my gardening gloves and then step inside.

I'm barefoot and my feet pitter-patter against the worn wood floor.

"Is that you fussing, Jamie?" I ask my little girl. The moment we drove away from the compound I stopped calling her Harmony, the name her father gave her, and I started calling her Jamie. After her father, of course.

I sit on the single rocking chair in the house. The wicker seat had broken, but I patched it up and made a cushion for it. Thankfully I remembered my sewing kit and several yards of fabric when I packed the van.

I've also made curtains for the window. I know it could be seen as silly, to be setting up shop here like this, when the truth is I am trespassing, but I've always wanted to have a place of my own. I've never been able to do that as a sister-wife. I was the youngest of George's, and certainly not one with a very loud voice, considering the bedrest.

I lay my girl back in her bassinet. She'd only been napping for about half an hour, so I'm surprised she woke at all, but now that she's fed, along with her brothers, I bet she'll be out for at least a few hours. Then all three will wake up, crying again to nurse, but they'll be in bed for the rest of the night except for the feedings.

I look at the clock and see that it's 7:30, and a hint of sunlight still shines through the windows. I stand and shut the curtains, and then take my most prized possession, my guitar, and carry it out to the porch.

Sitting on the steps I position my guitar in my lap and begin singing the song that I always return to; *If God Only Knows*. The one that I will probably always return to. The song that means more now than it ever did. The song that has become my heart's offering to James; a way to remember him now that he is gone.

As I'm strumming, I hear a car come up the road, quickly. My hands start shaking immediately, fear rising in my belly. The lyrics, *God only knows what I'd be without you...* I don't want them to be true. I want to know who I am when I am alone, I want to be strong and courageous even if I've lost half my heart.

I blink back my fear as the car comes to halt. I stand, pulling shut the door to the cabin, the only protection I can offer my babies.

The car engine cuts off within a matter of seconds; I don't have time to run even if I wanted. But I don't want to—I can't leave my children.

And then the man gets out of the car. A big burly, muscled man with a beard and—and oh my God.

He is here.

He isn't dead.

God only knows what I'd be without you.

I don't want to know.

And now you are here.

And I won't have to know.

I'm running then, tripping over my legs and falling to the ground and lying at his feet and pulling him to me and I don't how this is real—

but it is. I touch his boots; they are leather and I cling to his legs and they aren't broken and I reach for his hands and they are rough and calloused and familiar.

He pulls me to him, refusing to let go.

And his eyes. Oh, his eyes. They are the eyes I see when I close my own at night. And his arms, they wrap around me, reminding me of the past.

And his lips, they find mine. And they bring me to the present.

The here and the now and our dream for a future.

His kiss.

His kiss.

It is real.

James is here.

And he is mine.

CHAPTER TEN

James

I pull her to me, she's a mess of tears and long flowing hair and sunburned cheeks and she's shaking.

Shaking like she saw a ghost.

"I thought you were dead," she says, pulling from my lips, sobs escaping her, her heart pounding so loudly I press my hand to her breast to steady it. Steady her. Touch her. Feel her.

She is real.

This is no dream.

This is destiny.

"I thought—" She covers her mouth, then she drops her hands and then they are on my rough face, over my beard, and through my long hair. "James, I thought you were gone."

I shake my head, pushing her loose hair

from her tear-streaked face. "I'm not gone, love, I'm here. I'm here now."

"It's been... so long, James. I thought..." She shakes her head, and I wrap my arms tightly around her, hating to see her broken, unable to believe I've found her myself. What on God's green Earth is she doing here?

I take her hand, leading her to a big oak tree several yards from the house, because where else would I lead this woman?

I explain how I was left for dead; how Jonah kept me alive. How we struggled for a year but I was determined to come back here and fight for her... only to find that she was gone. That the entire compound was a ghost town.

"But then I came to see Harper, and decided to come here, to my uncle's old cabin until I came up with a plan as to how to find you... and here you are."

"You found me." She covers her eyes as tears continue to escape her. "I really thought you were dead, James, and I had no one I could talk about it with. I grieved you... I wept for you... and here you are."

I pull her to me, kissing her again, softly. "Here I am." I cup her face with my palms, our lips brushing, she smells like a wood fire and fresh air, like earth. She smells like hard work and determination, but more than that, she smells free.

And she looks free too. Different than I've ever seen her. Her hair is loose, not tied in a long braid. She isn't wearing a blouse, buttoned to the neck, and buttoned at the wrists. She isn't in her regular hand-sewn skirt either, she wears nothing but a nightgown.

"James," she whispers, leaning into my hand, pressing my other hand to her other cheek. "Is this a dream?"

I shake my head. "This is us finally catching a goddamn break."

"Don't let go of me, James. Now or ever." She looks at me, asking me for a promise I wanted to keep before, but wasn't able to. I want to believe nothing could ever take me from her again, but I also know that sometimes life has a way of fucking you over.

Sometimes the fight isn't fair.

Still, in this moment, I choose to believe I will fight all her demons, protect her for always. Right now, I want to believe my love for her is big enough to conquer whatever may come our way.

So, I promise. And my hands find her hands, and our fingers lace together, and under the big oak tree, I kiss her hard. No more soft kisses tonight. The sun is setting and our need is deep, and our love—damn, that is fucking real.

"Make love to me again," she asks, her voice soft but clear. She knows what she wants. After all those years of holding back, of not giving in to me and the love I had for her—she is ready to claim what I always wanted to give. "Make all the bad things disappear, if only for just a moment."

Anything for my girl.

I find the hem of her dress, the sun setting and the warmth of the sunset casting a pink glow over us both. I pull it over her head, and she gasps as I do, the summer breeze washing over us, around us. Wrapping us up in a lavender scented puff of air.

She looks beautiful, more of a woman than I remembered. She looks fuller, more voluptuous. Her breasts look huge, her ass bigger, her tummy rounder—in a sexy, I'm-all-woman way.

"Oh, love," I tell her, running my hands over her perfect skin. Wondering how I got so damn lucky to show up here when I was broken down beyond measure, to find her here. As if waiting for me. "How did you end up here?"

She shakes her head. "Later," she tells me. "Save that story for after. Right now, I need you to take me away. Far, far away." The tears are back in her eyes, she needs me to help her move past this place of pain she is in. She needs to be brought somewhere beautiful—somewhere ours.

Her hands tug at my shirt as if she needs to see more of me. All of me. I tear it off, and her hands are on my bare chest. She finds the tattoo on my skin, *Cherish* and she traces her fingers over the letters.

"Not Abigail?" she asks.

I smile softly, groaning as she undoes my belt, pulls it off. Her fingers resting on the waistband of my boxers

"I don't know the name you want me to remember you by," I tell her. "Abigail is beautiful, and the name you had growing up... but you were Cherish when you finally gave yourself to me. It means something different because of that. The woman you were when you finally said yes... that is the girl who had my heart."

"I should never have waited so long," she says, blinking away tears.

"We can't go back. We can't live in a place of regret, Cherish. We can only live in the present. Look at what we have." I shake my head, incredulous at our second chance. "We have one another."

I pull her to me, not letting this moment wash over us unless our bodies are pressed together, unless her skin in on my skin, our hearts are beating as one.

Wordlessly, her hands run under my boxers, her fingers finding my hardened length, my jeans falling to the ground. I kick off my shoes and step out of them, my body against her body, both of us naked outside under the tree. Same as when I took her last, it's crazy to think we have come full circle.

She's not ready to tell me her story, and that I understand: stories are complicated, especially ones born from sorrow.

She thought I was dead.

Her body is soft, opened in ways it wasn't a year ago. And when I touch her skin, her breasts feel tender. When I slip my hand between her legs, her pussy is wet, open, willing. In the space of a year, Cherish has become a woman the way she wasn't before. My heart breaks for her, for whatever has been done to her body, her heart. Her soul.

But also, knowing whatever has happened to her has made her stronger, more resilient.

Here.

Now.

In my arms.

I tell her I love her because I do. I kiss her hard, needing to feel her mouth on mine, and her breath is hot, her breath is heavy.

In my arms, I lay her on the lush green grass, her long dark hair splayed out around her like she is a goddess of nature. She looks at me with swollen lips and wide eyes. Then takes my finger in her mouth and sucks it hard.

"You know what you want?" I ask her.

She pulls out my finger and presses my hand between her legs. She doesn't say a word but I know exactly what she wants. What she needs.

I kneel before her, between her spread legs, relishing in the sensation of her hands wrapping around my cock, stroking me as if this is something she's done every damn day of her life.

But it's been so long, too long. It's been fucking forever.

She touches me, and with her gestures, she asks me to touch her too. So, I do. My fingers run up and down her wet slit, her body telling me this is what she wants.

My cock is thick with her hands wrapped around it, and I groan in pleasure. Her eyes close, her mouth turns up to a smile. God, it's so good to see her so happy.

My fingers run over her, circling her clit, needing her now, and wanting this to last longer than our first time.

My fingers press inside of her, her tight pussy opening to me, asking for more, and so I give it what it wants. My fingers move inside of her more and more quickly, until her back arches, her knees go weak.

Her hand slips from my cock, and then her fingers are gripping the blades of grass beneath her, as my fingers move faster and faster inside of her creamy cunt. She is dripping for me, for my finger fucking.

She moans as I finger fuck her. I move deep inside of her, causing her juicy pussy to coat the grass beneath her, she squirts as I ride her cunt like it was made for.

"Oh, James. It's too much. I can't. My body doesn't−"

My girl doesn't know what she needs. Her body has never been touched like this, but I already can sense that her body is going to love it. I press another finger inside of her, moving faster now, my thumb running over her exposed clit, throbbing under my touch.

I move fast inside of her until I feel the walls of her pussy throb, aching for release as it showers over my hand, she comes everywhere. She's dripping; no, that's not what's happening. She's gushing. Her body has been pent up for far too long, waiting for this moment under the oak tree. There is nothing here but a black, star-filled sky, she and I. This is the moment we've been waiting our entire lives for. And now we have it.

Now we have one another.

"James, come in me now, come in me now," she begs. My cock is still so fucking hard, and I'm not gonna wait for her to ask me again. She knows what she needs, and I'll give my girl anything she wants.

I press my cock inside her, thrusting deep into her tight pussy. Her legs wrap around me effortlessly, her ass raised off the ground and my hands run up her stomach toward her beautiful tits. Tits that bounce with each thrust I give her. She steadies them with her hands, but I push her hands away. I want to see them move, her hard nipples, her creamy skin. But she shakes her head, barely enough for me to notice.

"What is it, love?"

"They're just tender." Her words are soft, muffled as I come inside. Ribbons of my manhood fill her up to her very core. Good, I want my come deep inside of her, filling her up with all I have to give.

"Tender?" I ask as I pound her perfection.

"Yes, tender."

I come in her, hard, and she comes too, moaning as we exhaust ourselves in one another.

I lean over her, my elbows resting in the grass, my hands pushing away her hair from her forehead.

"Are you okay?"

"Yes," she says, smiling. "It's just..."

"You can tell me. You can tell me anything. Is it that time of the month?" I ask. "Because I don't want you to feel like you have to—"

She shakes her head. "No. It's not that."

"Then what is it, love?"

"It's just—" She bites her bottom lip. "I think you need to come inside and see for yourself."

CHAPTER ELEVEN

Cherish

James is here. And I'm leading him to my stolen house—his uncle's cabin. I'm not sure when my messed-up life became a fairy tale... but today it did. It's like the universe is rewarding me for finally taking the risk I always dreamt about.

Rewarding me with the man I thought was gone from me forever.

He filled me under the oak tree and it felt like everything wrong in the world was suddenly right.

He holds my hand, marveling at us both being here, but my stomach is churning with anticipation, knowing what is through the doors of the cabin.

His children.

"I'm trying to understand how you ended up here," he says, squeezing my hands tightly as we pass my tiny garden, my beat-up van. "How long have you been here?"

"About a month."

"Why didn't you tell Harper you were here? You know Honor lives on this mountain now, too? Got herself married, even."

I shake my head. "I didn't know that... but I don't want anyone to know where I am. You know how the church is... what if they come looking for me?"

"We could go to the cops."

"No, James. I don't want that mess in my life..." But really, I'm not thinking about me. I'm thinking about the babies. If I rat out George... who will come after me? It's too dangerous.

"You need to use your voice though, make sure no one—"

"James," I tell him, stopping at the base of the small porch. "I made sure nothing bad happened to my family by living like I did."

"Family?" His eyes narrow. "What does that mean?"

I push open the front door, a finger pressed to my lip. Nodding toward the bassinets in the living room.

"You're a mother?" James's face goes white. I know this is going to be a lot to take in... when he pulled up here tonight he had no idea I would be here, waiting.

And now... now he is going to discover he is the father of three.

"I had triplets three months ago."

James runs his hands over his beard—a look that is taking no getting used to. He looks so handsome like this: rugged, strong and capable. I know with all my heart that he is going to be an incredible father.

When I look back at him, though, I see a sadness in his eyes I wasn't expecting.

"You had George's children?" he asks softly, his hand finding the small of my back.

"Oh, James," I say, shaking my head, giving him the slightest of smiles. "No, these babies are yours."

He draws in a deep breath and steps closer to the sleeping babes.

"How can you know? Surely you and George..." James lets his sentence drop and I'm grateful. I don't want to talk about lying with George either.

"I did what I had to do, but look at them, James. These children are yours."

He kneels before the bassinets, his hands on the rim, looking down at his children for the first time in his life.

Our boys have hair as dark as a raven's wing, eyes that dark, too—mirror images of me. But his daughter, Jamie, has hair as light as the sun, eyes green as the grass. His double. They're sleeping now, but I know when he looks in her eyes, he will know what I knew the moment I held them in my arms: they are ours.

James pulls in a sharp breath as I lift Jamie from the bassinet, swaddled tight, her little hands tucked beneath her chin. I hand James his daughter and there are tears his eyes. "Triplets?" he asks in wonder.

I can't hold back the grin now, and why would I? "Crazy, right? Just like your sister."

James blinks back tears, lifting Jamie closer, kissing her little nose, her cheeks, her lips. Breathing her in and staring at her perfection. My heart has melted, seeping toward my family.

He sets down Jamie and picking up Jacob, then Andrew, memorizing their faces. We stand there for what feels like hours, staring at our children, he unswaddles them looking at their fingers and toes, marveling over their existence. Watching him fall in love with our babies is the most beautiful thing I've ever witnessed.

As they stir, I bring them, one at a time to my breast. Nursing them in the rocker, James is transfixed by us, by his family. He begins humming the Beach Boys song, *Wouldn't It Be Nice* as a lullaby, and that's when I lose it. My tears begin to fall for the time he has lost, and they have lost. For the moments he has missed.

But it's only been three months... and the truth is, I thought it was forever.

I thought he was dead, but he is here, his voice cracking, tears in his eyes, over the lyrics that mean so much to us both. And somehow his voice is more soulful, raw—real—it's as if all that we've been through has made him more of a man than I thought possible. His beard is rough, but his heart, it's still soft.

He's always been soft to my hard, the wide-open to my closed-door heart.

"It's like those lyrics were written for us," I tell him, rewrapping Andrew in his blanket and lying him in his bassinet. The babies are all fed, and back to sleep. "I haven't heard you sing in so many years."

"I lost my voice when you...."

I close my eyes, knowing they'd be cloaked in regret. "When I refused to leave with you when we were eighteen?"

He nods, walking toward me, and pulls me to stand. "You came out here all alone, with them?" he asks, his arms around my waist, my cheek resting on his chest.

I know I need to tell him my story, hard as it is to tell. It is time.

I take his hand and lead him to the bed I have made on the floor with all the blankets and comforters I had packed. He takes off his boots and pulls me to him, he's watching me as if I am something fragile. What he doesn't know is that right now, I am the strongest I have ever been. Stronger than I ever thought I'd be.

So, with that courage, I tell him the story. I detail the marriage vows with George, how the sister-wives dressed me in white and slipped the gold band on my finger and stood with me before Luke, our pastor. How I stood frozen, the shell of who I had once been, my heart wrecked over his death, unable to grieve.

I tell him how after, I went to the bathroom and threw up in the toilet, terrified of the night to come. How all I wanted was him.

How all I wanted was *him*.

How all I wanted was him, but he was dead and I was left alone.

And how I slept with George, but that it never felt real.

Because the only real thing I knew was gone.

I tell him about the months of sorrow, not being able to show my heartache over losing him to anyone for fear of what may happen to me.

When I realized I was pregnant, I knew immediately that I was carrying his child. I refused to believe George could ever fill my womb. How I clung to his memory as our babies grew and I how I was stuck in bed—but how that was better than anywhere else I may have had to be.

During the pregnancy, I resolved to leave as soon as the babies were born; as soon as I was strong enough to leave the compound with them.

And how the church planned on leaving anyway. When I tell him about the day of my escape, sick at the memory, he pulls me to him, and I lie across his chest, his head on the pillows, and I realize I have never been in a bed with him. That tonight is the start of a new sort of life.

"Where did they go?" James asks.

I sigh. "Not sure, George told me Montana... but I don't know any more than that."

"Those fuckers should have to pay," he says, anger in his tone. I've never heard that from him before. He has always been the grin-and-bear-it kind of man, an anchor in the rough seas of life. Not shaken. But now, now he is charged with something different.

I pull up and look at him. "Can't we leave it all behind us? We're together now. It's all that matters."

His eyes are hard, and the day has turned to night and suddenly everything that should be bright and hopeful feels covered in something dark.

"Those men should pay for what they did to you."

"You mean what they did to you and Jonah?" He was the one with broken bones, left for dead.

He shakes his head. "No, to you. I should have taken you from that place before it ever came to that. You say you spent a lifetime being scared—well I was scared too, in ways I've never admitted before. Dammit, Cherish. I should have taken you away and shielded you from this mess. I failed you." He buries his face in his hands, but I refuse to let him think this way.

I pull his hands down, straddling him. Looking deeply into his eyes with intent, blinking my tears away.

"Listen to me, James," I tell him. "You are the man I love, the man who made me a woman and a mother. The man who saw something in a sad little girl and wanted to make her world shine like the stars. And I refuse to let you beat yourself up over the past."

He shakes his head, my tears falling down on his cheek, the salty pain covering us both. He cups my face with his hands, refusing to let go. Just like he's refused to do forever.

"If you want me to forgive myself, you need to forgive yourself too," he tells me. "We both need to let go of the shit that holds us down.

We both need to move forward without regret. Without the past, we wouldn't have this present. And baby, I wouldn't trade this moment for a goddamned thing."

He looks over at our babies, then he looks at me, and he kisses me.

He kisses me until the hurt I've buried deep down surfaces. As our mouths part, and his tongue finds mine, the pain rises like a force, like a spring of water that cleanses us both, washing away the parts of our story we are ashamed of.

Making us whole.

CHAPTER TWELVE

James

She pulls up her nightgown, slipping it over her head, her full breasts even more beautiful now that I know she is a mother, her fuller figure a fucking altar I want to worship at, knowing what it has been through to bring our children into the world.

Cherish was never like other girls, and now, through her tears, I see she isn't like other women either. She feels everything so deeply, yet holds so much back, but now that she feels safe with me beside her, her walls crumble, and she opens herself to me—offering me all she has to give.

Her hands find my cock as she straddles me, my fingers running over her bare pussy. She's so sweet, and wet, so fragrant and tempting. I bring a finger, covered in her come, to my mouth, wanting to taste her. She is fucking spun sugar and I want another piece of her cunt-candy.

"James, when you touch me I forget to breathe..." She laughs. "Is that bad?"

"If it's bad, then I'm going to hell, love. Because baby, when you touch me, I forget where I am."

She leans over me, lifting her ass, letting my hard cock fill her creamy pussy. She sinks onto me, whimpering in pleasure as she does. Her body rocks over mine, and for just having a set of triplets she is still nice and tight like her body was made for mine.

She moves faster, and my thumb finds her clit, letting her revel in the pleasure of being touched and fucked at the same time. I've only ever been with her, but it's like I know how to work her body over. Like I was made for her in the same way she was made for me.

When she comes, she moans, and I cover her mouth, knowing how hard she worked to nurse and put those babies to sleep. Our babies.

I'm a father. And I am going to make Cherish my wife the first chance I get.

I come in her too, hard and fast, filling her the way I did under the oak tree, knowing I am going to take her again before the sun rises. Knowing I need to run my fingers over her ass, filling her up from behind. She is my gentle flower that is finally in bloom. I want to examine her petals, let her take hold of my stem.

She falls against my chest, exhausted from the talking and the fucking, and when I wrap my arms around her, I sing her to sleep. The song on my lips, one I know she loves: *Don't Talk. Put Your Head On My Shoulder.* The Beach Boys were always her favorite, and when she begins to breathe heavily, her body cradled in my hold, I know I picked the right one to put her to sleep.

———

The next day, I realize just how hard my love has been working doing this on her own. She's nursing these babies around the clock, in between changing cloth diapers, hand washing them in the boiling water, hanging them to dry —it's a full day's work—and she hasn't even fed herself. I notice her stomach rumbling, and ask what she's been eating.

"Canned beans and veggies." She points to her makeshift pantry. All home-canned goods—

which is impressive, but she's burning through so many calories a day just feeding our children.

"You need some meat on your bones, woman. Some eggs at least."

"If I go to the store I'll raise a lot of questions. Like, why is a woman with newborn triplets alone in the middle of nowhere?"

I nod. "I get that, baby, but I hate seeing you this way. Half-starved. And we need some tools. Do you even have an ax for firewood?"

She scrunches up her adorable nose. "No, I've been gathering sticks for kindling, for boiling water when I wash the diapers."

"Baby," I tell her, holding a cooing Andrew in my arms. "We're gonna need some more supplies."

Cherish folds her hands over her chest. "You think I need a man to survive? I've been doing just fine on my own."

"I know you have, this set up is impressive as hell, considering you already have so much on your plate. But let me go to town, buy some tools, talk to Jaxon about getting the utilities turned on out here. Hell, there's an ancient stove and fridge—you just need the power turned on. You're roughing it more than you have to."

"I've been a squatter, James, I couldn't

exactly call the utility company. I'm on the run, remember?"'

"You *were* on the run. You aren't running anymore. Jaxon already told me he has a job for me, so that's covered. We can fix this cabin up real nice, and hell, once we add another few bedrooms on the back, it will be home we can really live in. I can do that in no time."

"Nothing is ever that easy for us, James."

"It's different now. Now we are free from the past, remember? And when I'm in town I'll also find out about a marriage certificate."

Cherish purses her lips. "Is that a proposal?"

I shake my head. "Not officially. I need a ring first, for that." I pull a guitar pick from my jeans pocket. "But for now, take this and know I have been preparing for our life together for as long as I can remember."

She leans over and kisses me. "You better get me some carbs when you're in town too, forget the eggs and bacon. I want a donut and coffee. With cream." Her eyes light up at the thought.

I kiss her back. "You'll be okay up here while I go get some stuff?"

She smiles. "I've been here for a month, hanging on. I'll be okay for a while longer."

"I'll stop at Jaxon's and tell Harper to come over, is that okay? I'd feel better if you weren't alone."

"Okay, baby," she says, kissing the guitar pick, and slipping it into her skirt pocket. "I'll be waiting for you, now and forever."

I kiss her again, then the heads of our three babies, feeling like the goddamn king of this mountain. I have my woman, our children, and a place to make a home.

Now that we are together nothing can stop us.

CHAPTER THIRTEEN

Cherish

I'm laying the babies down in their bassinets when I hear a car rumbling down the driveway. I look up, surprised that Harper could be here so soon. It seems as if James left less than 15 minutes ago.

My eyes sweep over the babies, and even though I'm surprised someone is here, more than anything I feel content—maybe for the first time in my life. Because it feels like my babies are going to be okay. They are safe, wrapped in their little cocoons, sleeping contentedly.

My feet are bare and the air is warm. But when I step outside, the feelings of safety vanish immediately. I pull the door tight, as tight as it can go, and I wish I had a key so I could lock it. Because what I see is terrifying.

I know that car, and I know the man getting out of it. And I know he has come for me.

He's not alone.

Behind him, there are men from our church—*his* church. Not mine. I've moved on, I let go of those demons and I'm walking in the light. I walked away from their oppressive chains—but here is George and the elders. They don't belong here.

There's only space for love on this mountain. True, pure love. The love I have in my heart. And I will George to leave, to turn away and go.

But he has other plans for me. I blink hard, imagining him away, but when I open my eyes, he's still there.

He walks closer, close enough to see my eyes, I know what is to come.

So, I do the only thing I can manage.

I run. I throw my body through the front of the door, the idea of him penetrating the space where my children sleep unfathomable. He bangs his fists on the wooden door and my body leans against the back side, bracing myself in the frame, wanting to keep this monster out.

"Open the door, Cherish," he bellows.

The tears sting my eyes but I'm not crying for him. It's the fate of my children that worries me.

"How did you find me?" I ask through the
door. "How did you know I was here?"

He laughs, kicking open the door and
pushing me aside. When he pulls out a gun,
holding it much too close to me, I know the
worst is yet to come. The other men I recognize
create a circle around me and I don't move.

James has just got his family back. George
can't take his flesh and blood. Our children were
born from something beautiful, and I won't
allow them to go somewhere so wicked.

"That stupid boy, coming back and looking
for you. Dumb enough to mention it in town.
Dumber still to come back to the compound.
He thought we were all gone, but like hell we
were. Of course, Luke has people watching the
place. James doesn't seem to understand the
game he's playing."

"You followed him to find me?"

George shakes his head. "I got a call
yesterday afternoon from these friends of mine
at the compound." George looks at the men
with him. "Telling me the boy was looking for
you."

"Where were you? Did you go to Montana?"
I ask.

"Think I'm going to tell you that? Like I
could trust you with that information after you
betrayed me?"

"If I betrayed you once, why would you trust me? Why would you force me to—"

"Because the Lord gave you to me. There is no question about where you belong. You belong in my house. In my bed. As my wife. Not with some piece of shit boy who thinks he's a man. I paid for you—you're mine."

I shake my head, wiping my eyes with the palm of my hand. Refusing to cry over George's words.

His words try to break me, but I've already been broken and beyond that, I'm already rising again. I'm a phoenix, born from the ashes of his own making and I'm not going to stand here and walk across fire for George.

No.

The only person I'm going to go to the flames for is James.

For our babies.

But not George. Not now, not ever.

"I'm not coming with you. You can't make me."

George laughs in my face, his breath as sour as it ever was. His hair gray and his body week. But he's holding a gun.

And I'm only holding my heart.

He has the power to kill me. And after what they did to James, I don't doubt they'll do it if they see fit.

But they will not take my children.

I can be strong. I can be strong.

I *am* strong.

"I will make you do as I say. You're coming back to the compound and you're going to be taught a lesson."

"Don't do this, "I beg. "I'll never love you."

"No one is talking about love. We are talking about the Lord's will. You are mine, dammit. And in God's name alone I claim you as such."

I'm shaking now, my hands trembling, my bare legs threatening to collapse.

I will not fall.

I will not.

The gun is to my head, and the babies must sense my fear because they start crying, all of them at once.

The babies. My precious lambs. Hollering like wolves in the night.

"These babies aren't coming with us," George says with disgust, the spittle from his mouth flying. "I knew they were never mine. But I wasn't going to say anything around the other sister-wives."

His words prove to me what a coward he is. What cowards all these men are. Paying for young virgins, and claiming it's God's will.

"Then you already know. You know I don't love you."

"I already told you, this isn't about love. This is about what is right. And you are rightfully my property."

I'm glad he realizes the babies aren't his. I don't want them to come in that van with me. Because if they do, I don't know if they will ever come back.

I couldn't bear that, to have them ripped from their father.

"Just take me then," I tell him, falling to his feet. This time I let myself fall because it's my one chance of saving the babies from this cult.

George pulls me up by my hands, dragging me from the cabin. Slamming the door. Shoving me in the van.

And then, before I can stop what's happening, we're pulling out of the driveway, a blindfold is wrapped around my eyes, my wrists bound by rough rope. The tires peel out, spraying mud behind them, and carry us down the mountain.

My heart. My heart.

I thought it had broken so many times before but I didn't know what heartbreak was.

My babies. My James. They are my everything.

I have none of them.

This is worse than death.

This life I'm being led to is worse than it was in the past. Now they are going to make me pay.

James barely made it out alive when they punished him.

I don't know if my fate will be better or be worse.

CHAPTER FOURTEEN

James

The fact that I have triplets is astonishing—this is more than coincidence. This is mother fucking destiny.

Harper and Jackson can hardly believe it when I tell them Cherish had been up here all along over the last month with our children. Harper smacks me, tells me to stop messing with her.

She laughs and says there is something about this mountain that makes babies come faster than any other place on Earth. I don't think she's exaggerating.

When I explain that I'm not messing with her, she says she plans on coming up right away.

Jaxon smirks. "Holding those newborns better not give you baby fever."

Harper sticks a tongue out at her husband,

scrunching up her nose. "We'll just see about that," she says, her words telling everyone who's the real boss in their house.

I tell her I appreciate it, considering I have a handful of errands to deal with in town and don't want Cherish to be alone.

As I make my way down the mountain road, I think about all the things that need to get done today. My main goals are to get the phone line and electricity turned on, we may live in a ramshackle cabin, but we don't need to live like hillbillies.

It doesn't take more than twenty minutes to get to town, and thankfully both the phone company and power company turn out to be quicker errands than I had thought they'd be. After I finish there, I stop at the market—I need to get some real food in my woman's belly. She's been up here alone for a month, living on powdered milk and shit. It's time for her to be fed.

As I drive back to the cabin, I think how I'll work weekends and fix the cabin up right for her. For us. And I'll take Jaxon up on his offer for a job as well. Between that and my savings, I'll be able to care for my family.

I can't wait to walk through the door, and see my sister and Cherish together. With my errands done, I drive back up the mountain, ready to fry some bacon and gets some pancakes going on the griddle.

When I pull up to my uncle's cabin, a grin spreads upon my face. I see Harper's fancy ass sprinter van parked next to Cherish's stolen vehicle.

I'm glad Harper could come up and keep Cherish company, I'm guessing they have a lot to catch up on. They go way back, we were all raised in the same church, kept company with the same people. And I'm hoping that the two of them can become friends. Maybe Harper can introduce her to the other women who live on the mountain—and I know seeing Honor would be good for Cherish too.

Before the car's in park, Harper is running toward me, fear on her face.

"Oh my God," she cries. "I've been trying to call you but my cell didn't have service. And I couldn't just leave. I just—"

"Whoa, sister, what are you freaking out about?"

"She's gone!"

"What are you talking about?" I grab her hands and try to steady her. "Where is Cherish?"

"That's what I'm trying to tell you," Harper cries. "She's gone. I went looking for her and

but can't find her anywhere. I just don't understand. Her van is still here. The babies are—"

"Where are the babies?" I ask. "Where are
my children?" Everything inside of me seizes.
No, this cannot be happening. Not now. Not
when everything was just beginning to make
sense.

No. No. No.

Goddamnit.

"The babies are here," Harper says, trying to
soothe me. "The babies are fine--"

She shakes her head, covering her face. "The
babies are sleeping in their bassinets, but the
door was swung wide open. She wouldn't have
left. But look in the driveway." She points
behind me and I turn to look.

That's when I see the tire marks in the soft
mud, obviously new. Someone peeled out of
here. Fast.

"We need to call the cops. Now," I tell
Harper. "The church must have come back for
her."

"How would they know?"

"I don't know, Harper," I shout—louder than
I should. The last thing I want to do is startle
her or the babies. But I'm torn up. "Go home,
get Jaxon in case anything shady happens. I'll
call the cops."

"Of course, but I can't leave you here."

We walk to the cabin, the babies whimpering, and I immediately pick one up. Andrew, I think. But I just met them last night. I rock him, immediately realizing he needs to be changed. And I realize they are all gonna be hungry soon.

"If we don't have Cherish back in an hour we're gonna need milk for the babies," I tell Harper.

She just shakes her head. "Three-month-olds can't have milk. They need formula." She exhales. "James, I'll take care of the babies. You drive down the mountain until you get cell service and call the cops, okay?"

———

CHAPTER FIFTEEN

James

The cops are on their way, but before they get here, I grab that new ax I just bought at the hardware store, and I take it to the woods and start swinging.

My blood boils, my heart aches, as my worst fears have materialized.

Why the hell did I ever leave the house? Why did I go to town without taking Cherish with me? The one thing I didn't want to happen, happened. And it's all my fault. I swore I would take care of her forever, and what has just happened? She's gone.

She's been kidnapped. So, I swing that ax with all the rage and fury within me. Trying to understand what could've happened for her to leave the babies behind.

Unless the people who took her knew they

were mine. Maybe they didn't want the responsibility of taking care of our children if they were my flesh and blood and not George's.

I try to imagine Cherish leaving her children and I can't. Those babies are everything to her, and the fact that she had to leave them here breaks my fucking heart. I swing the ax again. Harder and harder until sweat is pouring down my face until the trunk of the tree is decimated.

Until my body is exhausted, and a cop comes up behind me.

"Hey, son, you okay?" he asks.

I spin around, looking him in the eye.

Am I fucking okay? I just lost my woman. She's gone.

Which is the story of our relationship.

But I can't just accept that anymore. Now I need her here. Now I need her with me.

I'm sure I look like a murderer to this police officer. Sweat pours down my face, my shirt sleeves are rolled up. I've been screaming my lungs out, shouting at the tree I've hacked to bits. I'm angry goddammit. But I'm not going to let anyone talk me down right now unless they can tell me where Cherish is.

"Do you know where she is?" I asked the cop. I step up right close to his face, needing to be heard, to be seen. "Do you know where my... Where my Cherish is?"

"I'm here because I'm responding to your call. I don't understand what's going on exactly."

"You don't know what's going on—*exactly?*" I ask, trying not to let my anger boil over, but that pot is just about done. "I told the dispatcher that the mother of my children has been kidnapped. And I need someone— someone to go look for her. Now. The men who have her, they're going to make her pay for what she's done."

Cop holds up his hands, frowning. "How about you put down that ax, son, and we can start at the beginning. What exactly has this woman done?"

"She hasn't done a thing. She is a prisoner. In a fucking cult. And she escaped, but they came back for her and—"

The officer cuts me off. "Listen... James, is it? Let's walk back to the police vehicle. We need to get the facts straight, all right?"

I drop the ax, willing to do anything he asks if it brings Cherish closer to me.

I follow him to his car, where another officer is speaking with Harper.

After I say my piece to both of them, they tell me, in no uncertain terms, that I am to come with them to the station to file a missing person's report.

"I can't leave my children," I tell them, angry

they are suggesting I leave any member of my family after what just happened to their mother.

"James," Harper says, "maybe it's best to just go with them, make sure all the facts are in order. I'll call Jaxon, he can go and sit with you until this is sorted." She touches my arm, urging me to calm down.

"Fine," I tell her. "But you need to go in that cabin and not let those babies out of your sight until I return, understood?"

Harper nods solemnly. "I'll take them to my house, all right? I have formula there, and disposable diapers. Is that all right with you?"

I nod, understanding her plan is better than mine—which is to grab these officers by their collars and demand they turn on their sirens and scour the mountain for my woman.

Then I walk inside the cabin to kiss my babies goodbye.

Swearing to be the father they need. A man who will get their mama back.

CHAPTER SIXTEEN

James

When I get down to the station, they start questioning me. As if I might be involved, and the reason Cherish is missing. As they survey the crime scene, the babies need to stay at Harper and Jax's for a few nights, and I crash there too. The whole time I can't sleep. I'm all torn up. Having the woman I want given to me and then taken from me more than once is more than I can fucking take.

And now I have our children. I look at our three babies, crying all the time because all they want their mama, but she isn't here. I try to rock them to sleep, but I don't have that touch that Cherish does.

I hate to say it, but I feel slightly better knowing that Harper and her cronies, like Rosie and Honor and Stella, can't do anything to calm the babies either. It's not just me. It's anyone who isn't *mom*.

But a few days later, I'm cleared by the police. My alibi was airtight, the footage at the hardware store proves I was there when Harper showed up at the house to find her gone. It doesn't change anything, though, Cherish is gone and there are no leads. I explain to the officers that Cherish told me the cult was headed to Montana to restart the compound. But Montana is a big fucking state. And it's not like I have anything else to go by. Of course, they promise to investigate, to follow any leads they may have. But I'm not holding my breath.

If I want to see my woman again then I have to find her myself.

Jaxon tries to talk me out of it: "You can't go looking for her when you have her babies," he says.

But they aren't just Cherish's children. "They are my children too, and they need their mother."

"They also need their father. And what are you going to do?" Jaxon asks. "Load those babies up in a van, driving up and down the interstate? It's a wild goose chase and you don't know where you're going."

"Isn't that what love is?" I shake my head, furious. I'm sitting out on Jaxon's porch—the last place I want be. I want to be in my cabin, with my children and my woman. Not here. I'm ready for my life to begin, but one thing after another keeps happening. I'm tired of not having what I've wanted forever.

What I'm so fucking close to having.

"You can't load the babies up in a van," Jaxon says, softer now. "I know you know that, but sometimes it sounds like you're getting some harebrained idea in your mind."

"She is half of my heart."

"Are you sure you're not following your cock?" Jaxon asks.

I push Jax back because he doesn't seem to understand what Cherish means to me. "No, I'm not following my fucking cock. How dare you to insinuate that?"

Jaxon raises his hands in the air. "Brother, I got your back, but you've only been here three days and already the mountain has lost its fucking cool."

"You're missing the point," I tell Jaxon. "It's not about what drama has been happening, it's that injustice has been happening. It's about where Cherish actually went and finding her. She's the mother of my children, what don't you understand?"

"I understand perfectly," Jaxon steps back. "But I also know that the cult is dangerous. If you find them, it doesn't mean you'll come out of it alive. Maybe you should—"

"Hell, no," I tell him. "No way in hell do I think you'd leave Harper for dead."

"The last thing your children need is both of their parents gone," Jaxon says, his voice low and gravelly.

Those are some words that hit fucking close to home. "I don't want that either," I tell him. "But I love her, Jaxon. And I have to find her."

Jaxon doesn't answer because he knows if he were in my position he'd do the exact same fucking thing. Anything to get her back.

"So, what's your plan?" he asks.

"I don't fucking know that yet," I tell him. "But I need to figure it out pretty damn fast."

—

Turns out my plan is one dead end after another.

The cops try to convince me that Cherish left of her own free will. They fucking suggest that maybe since she's already married to someone else, perhaps she needed to leave me with the babies to let go of those choices.

"But she isn't actually married to anyone," I tell him. "The cult is practicing polygamy."

"I understand you keep saying that, but there's no documented polygamy in the state of Idaho. So, if she's practicing, it's under the radar, and we can't do anything to prove it."

"But she isn't practicing," I yell. "She's forced into it."

"If we had a lead we could help you. The best thing you can do right now is move on. You know, sometimes, people don't want to be found."

His words sting, and I pray to God they aren't true. The idea of Cherish not wanting me hurts more than I expected, even knowing it simply isn't true.

The first chance I get, I load up the van, drive as far as I can toward Montana, about a nine-hour drive. I want to believe that maybe love will lead me to her like it had before when we both arrived at the cabin.

But it isn't fair to the babies to keep them in a car like that, and after one night at a hotel with three infants and one exhausted daddy, I know it isn't realistic to drive aimlessly looking for her with the babies.

Harper and her friends tell me the babies

will be fine with them, that they will be well looked after and that I don't need to worry.

As I kiss the heads of those three perfect babies, I swear on my life I will find their mother. Leaving them for the first time hurts like hell... but what choice do I have? Finding Cherish is the only thing that matters.

Jaxon and his buddies Hawk, Buck, and Wilder are all pissed as fuck too. The goddamn cops aren't doing anything besides filing paperwork. But we don't need that—we need vengeance.

We take turns, two at a time, leaving the mountain and the other women and children, and fly to Montana. When we get there, we drive for fucking hours.

We search, city by city, as many towns as we can fucking find, and look for her.

It's hard for everyone. I can't keep asking them to leave their families so I can find mine— but they refuse to stop looking.

The men on this mountain are nothing like the men back in the cult. They understand what it means to love deeply, to love well. To love your woman forever.

I won't stop searching until I have her in my arms.

But as the weeks turn to months, as the summer becomes fall, the leaves on the trees turning all sorts of brilliant colors—we find ourselves exhausted by a chase that is nothing but a dead end. It's hard to keep my head clear. I feel powerless to find Cherish—and I know she needs me.

I try to hold on to hope, but I know it's too much to keep asking my friends who have been here for me throughout all of this to continue at this pace. The rest of the men have growing children back home as well.

It's been five fucking months.

And the babies, they aren't just babies anymore. They are crawling and pulling themselves up. They're big enough to sleep through the night and we've come to understand one another. The four of us have been through it all together. First fevers and first teeth. First foods and first steps—for Jamie at least. Eight months old and that girl is moving—force of nature, that's what she is.

And dammit, it feels like it's all fucking slipping away. A life with Cherish. Five months is a long ass time. And winter is gonna roll in before we know it. Soon as it does, we'll be snowed in for months.

I call Jonah, filling him in. He's been here for me the best he can be, considering the distance between us, and as much as I'm grateful to all of Jaxon's crew for having my back—Jonah understands me better than they do—he's had my back and been with me through thick and thin.

"I'm just so goddamn restless," I explain. "I need to do something besides drive around, leaving the babies all the time. It's been months... and yet nothing. I'm no closer than I was before."

"You need to go find her yourself," Jonah urges. For some reason, his words ring most true —maybe because he is the one who has been through hell and back with me. He understands the power of these old bastards. How scared I am for Cherish's fate. He knows that the men at the compound will beat you with a shovel if they decide they don't like you—those fuckers don't need a gun.

Jonah tells me how he's dating some girl he met at a tattoo parlor—apparently, he's gotten all kinds of badass since I left. I feel like I need to be a little more badass myself.

"That's good, man," I tell him, trying to be happy for him.

"Enough about me," he says. "What's your plan? You can't live without knowing where she is."

"I'm gonna pack the van, just like Cherish did when she came out to the cabin. The babies are older now and can handle traveling with me. And there's no way I can stay put any longer."

The line is quiet for a minute. Then Jonah clears his throat. "I know you love her, James. But you can't pack those kids up and hit the road with winter coming soon. It's not like here in Miami. You aren't thinking straight."

"Fuck that, I have to go, Jonah. Don't you understand? I'm all alone. Trying to keep my shit together, but how the hell am I gonna do this?"

"Let me come and stay for the winter. You need someone to shoot the shit with, and hanging out with all those big, happy families is probably depressing as hell, considering."

"Considering Cherish is gone?"

I can hear Jonah sigh through the phone. "Exactly, man. Exactly right."

"No way, you have a life out there." I shake my head, though he can't see me. I'm mixing formula in a bottle, have Andrew in a carrier on my hip, and throwing animal crackers on the highchair tray for Jamie. Jonah doesn't need to be here for this. This is my life. Not his.

"I know you are done asking the other men on the mountain for help, and I know you'll never ask me for any—but I'm not asking. I'm telling. Let me come meet those babies of yours, and pour you some whiskey for getting through these last five months, all right?"

He doesn't let me talk him out of it, and he

tells me he'll be on the next flight coming to Idaho.

I look around the tiny cabin, shaking the bottle for Andrew, and thank God I'm not in this alone.

CHAPTER SEVENTEEN

Cherish

For so long I held onto regret. Regretting the choices I made—mostly that I wasn't braver, sooner. Knowing that one night with James might have to be enough for a lifetime.

After driving in a van for what seems like an entire day, we end up the middle of nowhere, at a compound very like the one we just left. Except this one is much more permanent. There were maybe a hundred of us before, not counting children.

But this place is much larger than that. There are hundreds of people here, and not just people from the Lord's Will Bible Church, we have now merged with a sister church of so-called believers. Apparently, our doctrine matched up enough that we can join forces without causing unrest.

They'd been here less than a month when I arrived, and everyone is still getting settled. At first, I hoped I would get lost in the shuffle. I don't know our exact location, of course, no one will tell the women. The people from Lord's Will were raised in the real world, home-schooled, and churchgoers, but for the most part, they are people like me. We haven't been living this lifestyle for very long.

The people here, though, have been living this lifestyle forever. How they've been going unnoticed for so long is beyond me. I catch on pretty quick that if this has been their way of life for a decade, no police officer is coming after them.

And certainly, no one is going to be coming after me.

The moment I'm pulled from of the van, George drags me to the church elders. Luke is here, still. And how that man is still holding his head high, after his three wives left him, is beyond me. But he's here, wearing his suit and tie, next to some men I've never seen before. Apparently, they are the pastors here, the heads of the church. And when I stand before them, I'm told to get on my knees.

I brace myself, terrified of what they are going to ask me next, already gritting my teeth, refusing to be the woman they want me to be.

Theirs.

But to my surprise, they don't ask me to sleep with them. They don't take off my clothes. Now I'm not saying they are good people, but they truly believe I am a sinner and I need to repent. They also believe that I wasn't holy enough to be returned to my husband. Yet.

I try to explain that I had been forced away from my children.

They told me losing my babies was a part of God's plan for me. Of course, this idea is ludicrous, but I know better than to talk back. So, I stop talking about my children at all, and I bow my head, and I pray to a God I've never understood, asking for salvation from this hell.

Somehow, somewhere, something hears my still, small voice.

They send me to the kitchen, where I am to work back-breaking labor, washing dishes and making food. I work 12 hours a day, no freedom, no privileges. And then, and only then, if I prove myself as a woman will I be allowed back into my husband's home.

Apparently, once I am at George's home I'll be allowed my own bedroom, have the honor of carrying his children, and the privilege of shopping trips in town. These men must think that will appeal to me.

That's the last thing I want.

I lived with George before, and his wives, and I know that even though I would be given more 'freedom', the cost is just too great. They're fools to think I would want more than a cot in the pantry. More than my hands in soapy water, washing dishes for the compound, day in and day out. This punishment is a privilege and they don't know it.

I'm certainly not going to tell them.

"What do you have to say for yourself?" Elder Luke asks.

"Forgive me," I beg, feigning sorrow.

A month passes this way.

I don't hear from James.

A month passes this way.

My milk has dried up, my babies will soon forget my face.

A month passes this way.

I miss my period.

A month passes this way.

My breasts are tender once more.

I throw up every morning like clockwork.

Another sinner, a woman who just started working in the kitchen a few days ago, presses her hand to my back when she finds me in the bathroom.

"Are you okay?" she asks. "Are you with child?" Her name is Grace, and she offers it to me.

I nod, hoping I can trust her. Hoping she won't betray me with this truth. I haven't lain with George since I've returned. And I already know my time is running out.

"I'm four months along. If I weren't wearing such a large dress and apron, everyone would already know."

Grace nods, understanding." You're not the first one this has happened to. I can help."

"You? How?" I look around the empty bathroom. "They are going to kill me when they find out I'm pregnant."

"It won't come to that."

"How do you know?" I've spent the last four months with my head down, so any gossip has been lost on me. I've hardly left the kitchen— the only time I did sneak off was to look for my father and siblings.

But apparently, they left when the compound moved. They aren't here, never even showed. And in some ways, I'm grateful, I want more for my brothers than what this place would have offered them... and I hope it means my father had some money left from what he was paid for me.

I can't think the worst about them. That my father may have abandoned them somewhere. More children I have let down.

"You need to hide this pregnancy for as long as you can."

I nod, agreeing. "And then what? Has anyone been able to sneak out?"

"It's not that easy. There are patrol guards here, watching who comes and goes."

"How do you know?"

"I grew up here," Grace tells me.

"What did you do, to get punished?"

She swallows, her eyes brimming with tears. "I tried to escape."

"Why wouldn't they just let you go?"

"Because the people here are monsters, Cherish. And that is why we need to be smarter next time. Why we need to make a plan that doesn't result in us returning right where we came from."

I look deep into her eyes. There's more to her story than she lets on, but it's not the time to push.

"Why are you helping me?" I ask.

"Because, Cherish, you know what it's like on the other side. But for me? I've never left this place. I need your help as much as you need mine."

"What will we do?" I ask.

"We are going to plan another escape, but this time, it's going to work."

Together, over the course of the next month, Grace and I plan each night when the compound is quiet, we whisper between the cots and figure out how we can leave.

Sneaking out still seems the surest bet.

"But it didn't work for you last time," I tell her.

"Yeah, but it will be easier with two of us."

It would have been easier, too, if my body would have cooperated.

I was on bedrest for the entirety of my last pregnancy.

This one seems no different. I know there must be more than one baby in my womb this time too because even at five months, I know that there is more movement than one fetus could produce.

And I start cramping.

The same way I did before.

I need to see a doctor, but I can't risk asking for one.

The night of the escape I tell Grace the thing I have been putting off for days.

"I can't go," I tell her. "I'm scared of traveling, hitchhiking, and sleeping in rest stops. I can hardly move as it is."

Grace swallows back any fear she may have. "I don't want to leave you, not after all this."

"I'll fake a fever for a few days if anyone asks. You have to go," I tell her, with the urgency that has grown in my chest every day since we started talking about an escape. "Go find my children. My man. You have to go to the mountain."

"Alone?" she asks, her eyes wide, her hands nearly trembling. Last time she tried to escape she was caught... but we know more now. We've been scouting the guards, watching when they take breaks, change shifts. The odds of us being successful are higher now, not to mention my time is running out. If I don't leave soon everyone will know I am pregnant. And I don't want to imagine what they will do to me if they find out.

Grace nods, putting on a brave face. But she's never been anywhere besides the safety of this compound.

"You can do it," I tell her, reciting the directions to the mountain, telling here exactly where she needs to go. "Take this with you," I tell her, setting the guitar pick in her palm. "And give it to James when you meet him. Because you *will* meet him. I know it."

CHAPTER EIGHTEEN

James

Jonah wasn't lying when he said he got himself a bunch of tattoos. He and I got our first ones together in Miami—I got *Cherish* on my chest, and he got a big ass whale across his. Since then he's covered himself in a dozen more and looks more hardcore than I know he really is.

Because damn, he can put the babies to sleep about as well as I can.

He's been here a week, and already he and I have set to adding an addition to the house. When Jaxon and his buddies found out, they told their women to come get my babies and helped us get the addition built in no time.

With their help, we build three simple bedrooms off the main cabin. Though it's not technically mine--my father was given it after my uncle died-- we all figure if he ever thought about showing his face back on this mountain he'd be running for the hills, knowing we all had plans to whoop his ass.

"It means a hell of a lot," I tell them, knowing everyone has taken time off work to help me put this house in order. The babies will appreciate it too—having enough room for them to learn to crawl and walk is a true blessing.

But it's hard to start counting them.

Stella, Wilder's wife, insists on helping decorate. She used to be an interior designer and knows what she's doing. She picks out paint and fabric, and while the men are putting the finishing touches on the cabin remodel, she enlists the help of Josie, the girl who works at Rosie's diner, to help her get the main cabin room together. I hardly recognize the place.

She's turned the place into a calm and comforting oasis. How she managed to do that with all the gear a set of triplets require is beyond me. She even turned a small nook into a space for Cherish, believing she will return one day, somehow. Cherish's guitar is hanging on the wall, and she framed a print with lyrics from a Beach Boy's song and added a plush blue chair where I can imagine the love of my life curled up, strumming her instrument.

"Thank you, Stella, I know you've never met her, but the fact you'd go to all this effort—"

She cuts me off. "You know, when I met Wilder he had just taken in his brother's newborn twins. I have a soft spot for a man who puts everything aside to take care of his children. What you've done the last five months is nothing short of incredible." She wipes a tear from her eye. "Your babies are all so precious, and we just hate that this has been the reality for you all."

Her husband, Wilder, comes up behind her, looking at me, and he smiles. "You making my woman cry?"

"I was just telling James that he has the sweetest babies." She pushes out her bottom lip. "I miss mine being so small."

Wilder scowls playfully. "Woman, you have plenty of babies in the house."

She shrugs, pouting. "But none so tiny. Mine talk back now."

"You're not allowed to get baby fever, you understand," he tells her, wagging a finger at her, with a smile on his face.

Stella raises an eyebrow. "I know ways to make you change your mind."

"Uh, I think I'm gonna go check on Jonah," I tell them, not wanting to be here when they start getting all hot and bothered.

Stella twists her lips. "He's busy."

I narrow my eyes. "What's he doing?"

"He went to town with Josie. Something about needing supplies?"

I shake my head, having noticed the way Jonah looked at that waitress. She's a sweetheart but damn, she has that glazed over look that screams *I want a baby, and I want you to be the daddy*. There are too many kids up here, and she's been helping babysit all of them—I won't be surprised if she has Jonah wrapped around her finger by the end of the winter.

That weekend, the cabin is done. With more space to spread out, we've put the babies in their own cribs in one bedroom, set up another room for me, and the third is a guest room where Jonah is crashing.

Today, though, Josie came over to hang out on her day off. She and Jonah are in the babies' room installing a closet organizer and I'm loading the dishwasher. It's like we're a big happy family—except we are missing the one person I need for this to work.

I close the dishwasher door, and head to the record player, I ordered it online, a copy of Pet Sounds too—Cherish's favorite—and let the song *Let's Go Away For Awhile* fill the low rafters of the cabin, and I add a few logs to the fire-place. I'm guessing a winter snowstorm is going to come in the next few weeks, and the chill has already come through.

I'm handing Jacob, who's in a Jump-a-Roo in the living room, a teething biscuit when there is a knock on the door.

Frowning, I walk over and pull it open, not expecting anyone, and not having heard a car pull in.

When I open the door, I find a young woman who looks like she's seen better days.

Much better days.

She wears a long dirty dress, a bulky winter coat about three sizes too big, and a pair of sturdy boots, and her hair's in a long braid.

"James?" she asks, her eyes filled with exhaustion.

My eyes narrow. "Who are you?"

She swallows, then reaches into her coat pocket. "I'm a friend of Cherish. And she asked me to give this to you." The woman unfurls her hand, and in her palm, is the guitar pick that has crisscrossed the country.

"You know where Cherish is?" I ask, my hands shaking as I take the pick from her.

She nods. "Yes. And she needs you. Now more than ever."

CHAPTER NINETEEN

James

Josie, Jonah, and I each have a baby in our arms. The woman who looks like a train wreck personified stands before us, all of us slack-jawed and shocked.

"Where is she?" I ask, pacing the room. "Tell me, I have to go, I have to get her."

The woman nods. "I know. Cherish needs you. I hitchhiked here because she needs your help. I left last night and traveled all night. I'm just so tired. And so, so..." She covers her face, heavy sobs escaping her.

"Oh sweetie, let me get you some tea, and some food," Josie says, setting Jamie in a Pack n Play, and heads to the small kitchen and turns on the electric tea kettle.

Jonah and I eye one another anxiously, trying to understand the deal. "Where did you travel from?" I ask again. I can't just sit around here if she knows where my woman is. I need to go get her. Bring her home.

"In eastern Montana. It's about 11 hours from here, way out in the middle of nowhere."

"We've been going to Montana every week for the last five months," I tell her. "Where exactly were you?"

"A few hours east of Circle." She shakes her head as if trying to remember details. "The property is so far out, and I've lived there all my life. I didn't even know where I was on a map until I got in a car last night and asked the couple who picked me up for directions." She takes a crumbled piece of paper from her coat pocket. "This is the closest I could come to an address. The compound is off the grid, but there are a lot of us out here. At least six hundred."

Jonah whistles slowly, and I take the paper from her hand and then head to the hallway where I have a giant map of Montana, red lines drawn over the routes we've taken, the land we've scoured. We never made it to Circle, but we weren't too far off. We were looking in the right state at least.

"I gotta go get her," I tell them.

Jonah stands. "You aren't going alone."

Josie hands the woman a steaming mug of tea, casting a scowl at Jonah and me. I have no fucking clue what we did wrong, but Josie is letting us know there is something we missed.

"Sweetie, what's your name?"

Oh, I guess asking that would be the polite thing here—but I honestly don't have time for polite.

"Grace," she says, then biting her bottom lip, she looks at us worriedly. "Look, I understand you want to go find her, and you need to, but it's very dangerous there. You'll need guns, some sort of protection."

"I don't need anything but my own bare hands," I say as I turn to go to my bedroom and start shoving clothes in a duffel bag. "Can you stay here, Josie, with the babies? Call Harper, ask her to come too."

"Should we call Jax first? He can go with you," she says, walking toward my bedroom, worry stretched across her face. "James, maybe we should hear Grace out."

"I don't have time. And I don't need anyone's help. I know where Cherish is." I turn to Grace. "You said she needed me—is she in trouble? I mean, beyond the 'kidnapped by a group of psychopaths' part?"

Grace nods. "She needs a doctor. Soon."

My heart pounds in my chest. I remember when they tried to kill me, left me for fucking dead. If they have laid a finger on my woman—

there will be hell to pay. "What's wrong with her?"

Grace bites her bottom lip. "I'll let her tell you that."

I throw the duffel bag over my shoulder, ready to go. Ready to claim what is mine.

"Hell, no," Jonah says. "You can't go alone. That's insanity, James. We know better than anyone how insane those people are."

I slam my fist in my other palm. I don't have time or room in my head for their negativity. I have a singular focus: getting Cherish home. "Dammit, I have to go."

"Jonah," Josie says, reaching for his hand. "Go with him. He's not thinking straight."

"Maybe I'm not," I shout. "Maybe all I can think about is that I need her and I need her now. I look around my cabin, at my beautiful children, and I remember that when they were brought into this world Cherish thought I was dead—and for the last five months I've feared that she was. Now I know we're both alive, but that isn't enough. I want more than that for us, for our family. I want to fucking flourish. I want to put down roots, and I want to make this mountain our home."

I can't do any of that without her.

My words hit them hard. Josie wipes tears from her eyes, and dammit, so do I.

Jonah fills a duffel bag, Josie asks again if we will tell Jaxon where we are headed, says we shouldn't go alone.

But I don't have time to wait. I need to go now. While I know I said my bare hands would save me, I think it through and open the gun safe in the back of my closet. We're living in the wilderness and I have two .357 Magnums for protection. I add them to my bag and lock the safe back up.

Grace explains exactly where Jonah and I are to go once we get outside the compound. She tells us what fence to crawl under, what path to walk on—how we need to do this in the dead of night. She says people might be on guard, considering she escaped, but, who knows, maybe no one will have realized she is missing yet.

"And where do we go once we get through the guards?" Jonah asks, writing this all down on a piece of paper.

I grin, loving his optimism.

Grace explains where Cherish sleeps, tells us she's in a fucking pantry, sleeping on a cot. Imagining my woman like that tears me up again, but I don't have time to get angry about that now. I'll get my vengeance later.

Once Jonah and I understand the basic

layout of the compound, I thank Grace for all she has done for us.

I lean over and kiss my sons, kiss my daughter. Running my hand over my beard, I'm all torn up inside. I hate that I must leave this mountain, the place my children call home.

The woods that made a father out of me.

But I have to.

Cherish needs us and we need her.

"Thank you, Grace," I say again, as I pull open the door to go. "Thank you for coming here. For finding me. I owe you everything."

She shakes her head, her eyes filled with tears. "Go get her, and bring her home."

I swallow hard, blinking back tears like a baby—forget that—I let the tears fall like a fucking man.

Because tears don't make me weak. Tears prove I've got something to fight for.

Someone to live for.

And it's time I brought her home for good.

CHAPTER TWENTY

Cherish

My stomach is in knots. And it isn't because of the baby—thank goodness. It is because Grace has been gone twenty-four hours, and I don't know if she made it out alive.

Sitting up on my cot, I exhale, trying to remain calm.

I go to the bathroom, flicking on the light, I look at my face in the mirror, trying to remember who I am. It's been so long since I have seen my babies, my James. I press a wash-cloth to my face, trying to stop myself from hyperventilating at the thought of something happening to them.

Something happening to Grace.

If she was stopped... then my hopes of escape are narrow.

I can't think this way.

I run my hand over my blossoming belly, resting my forehead against the mirror, wishing I could float away to a world where there was sunshine and smiles and the promise of a bright tomorrow. Instead, I'm here, peeling potatoes and washing laundry and scrubbing floors. I'm here, attending services where I am lectured for hours on how to be holy.

I never used to know what to believe in. It took so long for me to believe in myself—my power to choose my own destiny.

But I waited too long before... and I fear I waited too long again.

I should have been the one to try and escape —I shouldn't have let Grace go for me.

When I press on my hands on my belly, I feel a kick.

A tear falls down my cheek. This baby needs its father.

I need my James.

I feel myself falling into the dark place I've spent so much of my life. I don't know if the right word is depressed, or prone to sadness— but I do know when things are hard it's hard to keep my chin up... it's hard to be bright when the world feels gray.

For so long I believed James would always be my sunshine.

But now he might just be a memory.

Closing my eyes, I imagine the life for myself that I've dreamed of.

If Grace was successful, James could be coming for me any moment.

I can't let myself spiral into a place of weakness again.

Not now.

I open the bathroom door, and head to my cot, slipping my dress over my nightgown, tying on my apron, and rebraiding my hair. I put on socks and shoes. There is no one else here, no one watching me.

When James comes—because I know he will —I will be ready.

Breathing deeply, I try to quiet the fear bubbling inside of me. And just when I think maybe I can get through this, I feel a sharp pain in my abdomen.

I press my hand to my stomach again, feeling the beginnings of contractions. The familiar pain of labor.

But this is much too soon.

I fall to my knees, eyes closed, head to the ceiling. Please let my baby be okay.

I start to pray for a miracle, but instead, I get a savior.

I'm on my knees, biting back the ache.

I've almost lost all hope, not believing he would find me.

But he is here.

"Cherish?" James whispers from inside the kitchen. My James. Here.

I gasp and call out his name. My deepest wish, my only desire—he is here.

He pulls off a ski mask, a gun in his hand. He reaches for me, but before I can fall apart in his arms—another contraction rips through me.

"I need a doctor," I tell him.

"What's wrong?" he asks, worry in his eyes, his hands refusing to let go of me.

"I'm pregnant," I tell him. "But it's too soon."

He lifts me into his arms, looking like a man on a mission. I'd be terrified of getting caught, but right now I'm more terrified of what will happen to our child if we stay put.

As we leave the kitchen, not knowing what we'll find—a SWAT team surrounds us.

Police lights blaring, officers with guns in the air.

James raises a hand and drops his gun.

A shot goes off in the dark and something warm blooms across me.

It's not me, though, that has just taken a bullet through the chest.

James.

My James.

He's been shot.

CHAPTER TWENTY-ONE

James

The trip to Montana was blurry eyed and Red Bull fueled. It was loud music keeping us awake and our eyes on the prize.

Cherish.

Finding her. Bringing her home.

Finally closing the chapter of our lives that took up more space than it should.

When we get to town Jonah and I stop and assess the plan, our route. We get some food, and buy a few ski masks, and get ready to crawl on our hands and knees into the compound. We park the car and hike in a little ways so as not to draw attention to ourselves.

Jonah is my backup, and with swift movements, we make it inside the compound. The property is large, but we've memorized the hand-drawn map from Grace and find our way to the kitchen. We don't see anyone, or hear anyone, and thank God for that. But as I walk through the back door, into the place Cherish supposedly lives, a sense of dread washes over me. It's all too good to be true.

The first thing I think when I see her on her knees, head back, chin lifted, is that she's praying. Which surprises me in and of itself. I stopped believing in the God of our childhood a long time ago. It's not that I don't believe in some higher power now... but it certainly isn't one carved from the cross our fathers wanted us to believe in.

No. If I believe in anything anymore, it isn't found on my knees with my eyes wide shut. No. What I believe transcends that small-minded idea of making women weak to feel powerful, it's more than judgment.

I believe in grace and I believe in forgiveness and, most of all, I believe in the power of love.

So, when I see Cherish on her knees, for a split-second I wonder if she and I have lost our way on the long stretches of distance over the years. We've had a singular afternoon, a much-too-short night... What we need is a lifetime, a repeat of our childhood. We need never-ending lengths of time to learn about one another, to laugh and grow as one.

But the idea that she and I grew apart is

fleeting because when she turns and sees me, I see she wasn't praying to the God of our childhood at all—she was praying for a miracle.

Cherish is in pain. Her beautiful face is written in it. Her hands shake, she clutches her stomach.

She calls for me and I come to her. I will always come to her.

With her in my arms, I leave the kitchen, hearing her plea for a hospital, understanding the urgency in her voice.

But before I can get her anywhere, we see police vehicles surrounding the premises, Jonah is in the distance with his arms behind his back. And I drop my gun, needing the officers to understand that I'm on their side. The lights are blindingly bright, but before I can shield my eyes, a shot fills the night.

And everything changes. The burn of the bullet is hot and cold at the same time. It sears into the right side of my chest, and I fall to my knees, gripping Cherish in my arms, and I find myself kneeling the same way she was only minutes ago.

Now I'm the one praying for a miracle.

"James," she sobs, "James," she cries. Her hands are on my face, and then she reaches for my hand, pressing it to her belly as blood pours from my body. "Don't let go. Don't give up. Feel this, it's your child. I'm carrying your baby, James, and you need to hang on. For us." She clutches my face again, staring into my eyes, as my world goes black. "No," she cries, as more bullets are shot around us, as I fall to the ground, and she hovers over me, her own body seizing as she cries out—because she is carrying her own pain.

On the ground, the night goes dark and Cherish looks into my eyes, wracked with sobs, ripping at my shirt. Begging me to hold on.

Hold on.

Hold on.

God only knows what I'd be without you.

CHAPTER TWENTY-TWO

Cherish

In the hospital bed, I wake with a start. Screaming before my eyes adjust to the light in the room.

"James?" I scream. I clutch the bed sheets. Blood on his shirt. A hole in his chest. His eyes closing. Being pulled away.

Kicking and screaming as my body contracted.

Body.

Contracting.

I press my hand to my belly.

Is my baby still with us?

I shake, terrified. Alone. Screaming for a nurse. "Help me. Help," I call. An IV is in my arm, I am attached to all sorts of machines.

"It's okay," a soothing voice tells me. But they don't understand. Nothing is okay.

"Where is James? I need to see him." I try to get out of the bed, but the nurse is at my side, pressing a hand on my arm, trying to settle me. But she doesn't understand. This can't be settled with a whisper, with a calming tone—I need James. James alone.

"I understand," the nurse says. Her nametag reads Betty but her name means nothing to me right now.

There is only one name.

One name.

One.

"Where is he?" I ask again.

Betty nods as if understanding. "He's in recovery."

I choke on my own tears, on relief. On hope.

I haven't lost hope.

"He's alive, then?"

Betty nods. "Yes, and if he hadn't had you in his arms, he might not be."

"What do you mean?"

"You gave him something to fight for, sweetie."

Betty checks my chart, lifts my gown, and adjusts a heart monitor on my belly.

A heart monitor. I look at the screen Betty is reading. My heartbeat quickens. "Is my baby alive?"

She raises an eyebrow, twists her lips. She's

an old woman, and with her sure movements and quick adjustments to my IV and monitor, I'm guessing she has delivered bad news a thousand times to patients.

She wouldn't twist her lip to tell me I'd lost my child.

Would she?

"What is it?" I plead. I need to know that my baby is okay, I need James back in my life, and I need to get home to my triplets.

It's been so long since I've seen their faces.

A sob escapes me, missing my children so deeply, having lost so much.

Scared I am losing more.

"Oh, dear, I didn't mean to worry you. I know you have been through so much. Everyone is talking about it. The local news channel has been reporting the story for hours. That compound wasn't just holding women hostage, they were practicing polygamy, embezzling money from the IRS and forcing teens into marriage."

I clench my jaw—knowing most of that. My shoulders sag, knowing so much of my life has been lost to a false religion.

"But Cherish, there is good that has come of your James rescuing you."

I lift my eyes to hers, searching for understanding.

"The FBI has seized the entire compound. Whatever horrible things were happening out there has been put to rest."

"How?" I shake my head still confused.

"I don't know all those details, dear." Betty shakes her head. "I shouldn't be saying all this anyway. Don't you want your happy news?" She taps the screen that is monitoring the heartbeat of my child.

"It survived?" I ask, already knowing it has. I feel the baby move inside me. "I was on bed rest my last pregnancy. But this time... I haven't been to a doctor and worried it was all my fault but I was so sca—"

"Shhh, it's okay. The heartbeats are strong—just like yours, and just like James's."

I bring a hand to my mouth, biting my knuckles in relief. "Thank God."

"But that isn't all." Betty raises her brow again.

"No?"

Betty shakes her head ever so slightly. "As far as we can tell, you must have been praying for a miracle."

I smile to myself, knowing that is exactly what I have been praying for.

"You are having triplets, again," Betty tells me. She pulls over the ultrasound machine and presses the wand to my belly. "See?"

Three little bodies light up the screen. It's beautiful, I never saw an ultrasound image with my last pregnancy, never having gone to a doctor besides our midwife.

"Triplets?" I can't help but laugh at the absurdity. At the wonder of it all. "And they are okay?"

Betty nods. "You'll need to be on bed rest, but if you can manage to do that for the rest of the pregnancy, you'll be able to go home. Though I'm sure the doctor will tell you all of that."

"And James?"

Betty pats my arm. "When he's out of recovery, we'll make sure the two of you—" She gets cut off. Another nurse pokes her head in the room.

"Betty, he's out of recovery." She looks at me and smiles. "You're one lucky woman everyone is talking about!"

I don't know if she is referring to the fact I was freed from a cult not once, but twice, or the fact I'm carrying triplets for the second time.

But then the nurse looks at me again. "The babies are lucky, of course— and so is the fact you are alive at all. But I was meaning you are lucky to have a man like James. He is one handsome—"

Now it's Betty who cuts her off. "Dana, that is completely inappropriate."

But I don't mind.

I know just how handsome James is.

I fell in love with him when I was just a girl, and under the oak tree he kissed my lips for the very first time and offered me his heart.

I didn't know how to take it then, how to hold on tight to the gift it was.

But now I know what I was unable to see when I was young.

A love like this is found once in a lifetime.

And I was lucky enough to find it with my best friend.

And I will never, ever, let go again.

EPILOGUE 1

James

She always said she was rain clouds—that I was the one who looked like blue skies and sun-tea. And maybe that was true before... but now?

No way in hell is that what I see.

Because when I look at her, in our cabin, with our three newborns swaddled, two in her arms, and one in mine—I see nothing but a radiant smile, her eyes beaming with pride. I see the woman I cherish, the woman I have and the woman I promise to hold—forever.

"Why are you looking at me like that?" she asks, her voice soft, her eyes bright.

"Because all I can think when I look at you is how goddamn lucky I am," I tell her, sitting beside her in our bed. I kiss the head of the son in my arms. She is holding both girls in hers.

"You haven't stopped complimenting me

since we left the hospital in Montana months
ago."

"You mean the night my life began for the
second time?" I run my finger up her bare arm.
She's in a tank top and leggings, her hair
recently chopped to a short bob—the first real
haircut of her life. I love her short hair—a literal
weight was lifted, sure, but a metaphorical one
too. She isn't carrying so much anymore.

She's learning she doesn't have to carry
anything alone, ever again.

She shakes her head, her hair swishing as she
does. "You're going to regret being so nice to
me. There's no way I can ever catch up to how
good you are to me. I mean, for months I've lain
in bed while you've watched Jamie, Andrew, and
Jacob. You've been on mom duty and dad duty
—and never once have I heard you complain."

I place the sleeping baby in the bassinet
beside the bed, and take the swaddled ones
from her arms and rest them beside their
brother.

"I've had help all this time. Jonah and Josie,
not to mention Grace." I sit beside her in our
king-sized bed, wrapping my arm around her.

Cherish nods. "I know. But still, I wish I
could make it up to you."

I cup her face with my hand. "Soon enough,"
I tell her, grinning.

She sighs, then bites her bottom lip. "The babies are two weeks old. But soon enough they will be two months old. And then," she says. "Then I will make it up to you plenty."

I kiss her lips, breathing her in, grateful to have her beside me. And of course, ready to take my woman hard and fast—but knowing we are going to need to take things very slow. We haven't slept together since she was rescued, the night I took a bullet; the night the FBI raided the compound.

After Jaxon got the story out of Grace—the day Jonah and I took off for my girl—they called the police. Apparently, the FBI had been looking for a location on the cult that the Lord's Will joined forces with. They'd been running a gun cartel for years, embezzling money too—and they were the ones who took a shot at me before the FBI took them all down.

The entire compound has been dismantled, families displaced—children taken into custody of the state—and for that, we are all grateful.

But Cherish was put on bedrest... so even though she was only five months along, and in other circumstances, we would have been able to enjoy the fact we were finally together—and whole—but we were forced to abstain for her health.

"Before we make love for the third time in

our lives, we have to take care of a few things though," I tell her.

"Oh yeah?" She narrows her eyes and suppresses a laugh. "Like make sure I'm on birth control?"

I grin. Six babies under two are plenty. But I shake my head because that's not what's on my mind. "I'm not talking about that."

"Then what is it?" she asks as I reach into my pocket.

I pull out a ring and hold it between my thumb and forefinger.

"I'm talking about you making an honest man out of me. About you becoming my wife."

She covers her mouth with her hands, tears in her eyes.

"It's about damn time, wouldn't you say?" I ask. "I've been in love with you since you made me mud pies when we were four. Since you offered me your song book when we were seven. Since we pinky swore we'd be best friend for the rest of our lives. I've loved you as long as I knew how to run, and Cherish, you are the only girl I ever wanted to chase. I want you to be my future, and I'm the luckiest man to have had you for the entirety of my past. As the Beach Boys would say, *we could be married, and then we'd be happy*."

She shakes her head. "I don't need to be married to be happy with you, James."

"But wouldn't it be nice?"

She laughs through her tears. "Yes, James. Yes, it would."

"So, you'll be mine?"

"Always. I'll always be yours."

I slip the ring on her finger and start counting down the days until Cherish is my wife.

EPILOGUE 2

Cherish

I wear a white dress and a veil. And I'm bare-foot—though not pregnant!

It's July, and our youngest babies are three months old.

And while I'm no virgin on my wedding night... James and I haven't slept together since our babies were conceived.

The doctor cleared me a few weeks ago... but we decided to wait.

After all, we'd already waited long enough.

I walk down the aisle in our back yard. Our property has a massive oak tree—because of course, it does. And there is no better place for James and me to exchange our vows.

Everyone is here. Jaxon and Harper of course. Wilder and Stella—who, bless her heart, decorated my new home with magazine-worthy perfection. There are Buck and Rosie, and Honor and Hawk. And everyone's children. At this point, there are so many, it is hard to remember which little goose belongs to whom.

This mountain may be jokingly called the *fertile mountain,* but I like to think about it a little differently.

The couples here, at my wedding, have committed to the thing that matters the most in this world. Family.

And so ours grow at a ridiculous rate.

The definition of a miracle is a surprising and welcome event that is not explicable by natural or scientific laws.

So, I don't call this place the fertile mountain—I call it the *Miracle Mountain.*

And I don't know about religion or God or what happens after this—my head and my heart still have a lot to unravel about all that... but I do believe in miracles.

God only knows what I'd be without you.

James is under the oak tree, guitar in hand, and he is singing *Wouldn't It Be Nice,* a song we learned together, the lyrics truer today than ever before.

The first time I heard his voice, I thought he sounded like a sunny day, and as I walk down the aisle toward him I know he doesn't just sound like a ray of sunshine—he is my happily ever after.

Jonah marries us, he went back to Miami after the dust settled, and came up for the babies' birth, and now he's here for the wedding. Everyone's trying to convince him to stay... we all know how Josie is pining for him still after all these months. Grace is up front here too, with our year-old triplets. She's not only been my faithful friend, but she's been our live-in nanny.

I smile, looking at the people gathered to celebrate my marriage. I would never have dreamed that they would be the guests at my wedding. There are all these burly men, covered in tattoos, but wearing the biggest smiles any man could ever have. All of us—the men and the women gathered here today have been through the wringer of life—we've been forced into situations that broke us and left scars so deep, we thought they'd never heal.

But love saved us. Every single one of us. And James promises to take me as to his lawfully wedded wife, to have and to hold, from this day forward, for better, for worse, for richer, for poorer, in sickness and in health, until death do us part.

I do.

I do.

I do.

When he slips a ring on my finger I consider his eyes and see the father of my children, my husband, and my best friend.

"You may kiss your bride," Jaxon tells him.

And James does. He kisses me hard, with promise. He kisses me soft, for the ways we've both been hurt. He kisses me deeply, knowing our love story began the day we met.

Then he picks me up and carries me to the house. The reception can start without us.

After all, we have some business to take care of first.

He carries me over the threshold, and the record player spins our favorite songs. He sets me down in our bedroom and reaches for my face again.

"I love you." He kisses me again, this time urgently.

And I kiss him back, needing more.

Needing all of him.

I unbutton his dress shirt, his abs a row of muscles and pure strength. I turn, and he unclasps my wedding gown, letting the white silk fall to the floor. I step out of it, and his mouth is on my neck, kissing me, reaching around and cupping my breasts with his hands.

My head falls back, onto his chest, and he unclasps my white lace bra, letting it fall away. My breasts are exposed, and he spins me to face him, his kisses trailing from my neck, past my breasts, until he is on his knees.

He tugs down my panties, my pussy greedy, not wanting to wait, and my wetness begs him to go faster. He listens.

He stands and I unbelt his pants, pushing off his boxers, our desire growing more fervent, the pent-up pleasure from months... years... rushing out of us. Maybe the rings on our fingers give us the permission we needed because we aren't waiting.

Life is precious.

A gift.

A miracle.

His cock is hard, in my hand, and his fingers press against my wet pussy. "I love you," I moan, as he fingers me softly, then harder, then I'm on my back, legs spread wide as he leans over me.

"I fucking love you more," he growls in my ear. This man who works with his hands, who lives and breathes these mountains, who isn't from here, but was made for this place—he is my mountain man.

Leaning over me, he runs his hands over my skin, my body tingling under his touch. I've longed for this moment for so long. I gasp, my body opening for him, having forgotten how big he is, how much of man he is.

How much I need to be filled by him.

"Damn, it's been a long wait, baby," he groans as he pushes deeper inside me.

"Worth the wait?" I ask.

"You are worth *everything*."

He isn't talking about sex being worth it... he's talking about me.

For so long, I didn't think I was enough for a man like James.

But he tells me with his actions that I am more than enough for him.

I blink back tears as he rocks inside me. My chest heaves as he fucks me the way my body was meant to be loved. Completely.

James was my first and he'll be my last.

He is my forever.

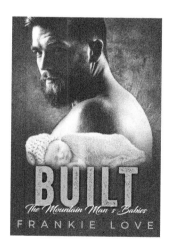

I pull into the diner of this small mountain
town, knowing there's only two things I want:
To put down roots and find someone to build a
life with.
And when I slide into the booth, the woman

who pours me a cup of joe is sweet as sugar and
warm as apple pie.
She serves me up a "Josie Special" and I know
she's made to order—the only woman for me.

My past is dark, too dark for a ray of light
like her.
But she cracks open the clouds and lets the
sunshine in ... she sees me as the man I can
become.

Her father wants me gone.
He thinks he knows all about me.
But he's wrong, and I'll do whatever I can to
clear my name.

For Josie. For our love.
For the life we will build together.

Dear Reader,
You're going to melt when you meet Beau
Montgomery—he's BUILT, if you know what I
mean. He's all man, all alpha—and all yours.
This mountain is full of babies, and he's gonna
make one fine baby-daddy—guaranteed!

xo, frankie

The Mountain Man's Babies:

TIMBER

BUCKED

WILDER

HONORED

CHERISHED

BUILT

CHISELED

HOMEWARD

RAISED

FAITHFUL

ABOUT THE AUTHOR

Frankie Love writes filthy-sweet stories about bad boys and mountain men. As a thirty-something mom to six who is ridiculously in love with her own bearded hottie, she believes in love-at-first-sight and happily-ever-afters. She also believes in the power of a quickie.

Find Frankie here:
www.frankielove.net

Printed in Great Britain
by Amazon